POKE CHECK

Harrisburg Railers, book 4

RJ SCOTT

V.L. LOCEY

Love Lane Books

Copyright

Poke Check (Harrisburg Railers #4)

Copyright © 2017 RJ Scott, Copyright © 2017 V.L. Locey

Cover design by Meredith Russell, Edited by Sue Laybourn

Published by Love Lane Books Limited

ISBN - 9781785646218

All Rights Reserved

Dedication

To my family who accepts me and all my foibles and quirks. Even the plastic banana in my holster. ~ V.L. Locey

To the Pens who have plenty of time to win some games. And always for my family ~ RJ Scott

* * * * *

With grateful thanks to Meredith Russell for her beautiful cover. Rebecca Hill for her editing and for making us look good. Rachel Maybury for sorting us out. And to our army of proofers for their hard work.

POKE
Check

— HARRISBURG RAILERS 4 —

RJ SCOTT &
V.L. LOCEY

Love Lane Books

ONE

Erik

In Sweden we have a saying, "*Det blir som det blir*".

Loosely translated, it comes out something like "whatever will be, will be", and despite some missteps along the way, I do believe that everything happens for a reason.

Like me, being here in Pennsylvania, when yesterday I'd been sitting in the yard in a San Diego winter with just a jersey and a thin jacket. Today there was snow. Lots of snow. And it was past cold and on to bitter when the wind caught you the right way.

"You might want to get a better coat," Emma said helpfully. She was my liaison to get me settled; she'd had me sign lots of forms, allocated keys and a key card, and reeled off a list of rules that apparently all the Railers players adhered to. "Like a thicker coat, maybe."

You think? I was shivering. The cold had seeped into my bones, and even though she'd explained as she did the tour that the East River Arena, only a few years old, had heating problems that were being fixed, I hoped to hell it wasn't this cold all the time.

And yes, I know I'm from Sweden, and a hockey player; I know I should be okay with the cold, but this Harrisburg winter was enough to freeze my balls off.

"A coat is on my list," I said, and gave her my best smile. She grinned back and tilted her head a little, just like my ex had done the night I'd met her, slept with her, and created a new life.

I love women, I love men, and if I'd been on the market then Emma, or indeed that Pete guy who ran security and who'd patted me down when I arrived, would have been on my radar. But I was so not on the market, and there was no way I was getting it on with anyone for a very long time.

My son was my primary goal, that was the truth, and behind him came hockey and winning the Stanley Cup. The pinnacle of hockey excellence, it was that single shining, beautiful, object that every professional hockey player wanted to win.

Not that I really expected the Railers to get it this year; they were an expansion team, new to the NHL, kind of raw, with a lot of potential.

They had a good group of guys in their farm team—young men who were being molded ready to move up to the Railers themselves. I was one of those in that feeder team. Not that I was young; twenty-seven is way past 'young' when you have eighteen-year-olds coming in and showing you how it's done. I'd expected to finish my time with the Carlisle Rush, or another AHL team that would take the chance on me, but no, things had moved so fast, injuries had happened, and here I was, up with the big boys.

And him.

As my agent said, the Railers were an exciting team, a new team, a team that wanted me playing the big games, and boy was I ready for that. I'd been drafted at eighteen, and since then, nine long years, I'd played AHL hockey. Not that that was essentially a bad thing, but still, I wanted to play for the cup. I wanted that ring, and the depth the team was creating was going to enable them to make that run. Hopefully with me hanging on for dear life and not fucking up too much.

"You're one of those skaters who grow into their skills, their bodies." That was what my agent pointed out whenever I lost the conviction that I could do any of this. "The boy has become a man," he had added, because he did that kind of thing where he sounded like Yoda but with the ability to get his words in the right order.

Emma stopped walking, and I nearly crashed into her. So much for my much-vaunted balance and awareness.

"This is one of our defensive coaches," she said, and waved a hand at a tall blond dude who stepped out of a doorway marked "Coaches", who you'd have to be a complete idiot not to recognize. "Jared Madsen," she added, just in case maybe I was one of those skaters who didn't know the world of people he played in.

"Welcome to the Railers," Jared said, and extended his hand. A defenseman turned coach, he was also in the middle of some serious issues about who he was dating. I mean, I knew that anyway, but Emma had spent a good thirty minutes challenging my conceptions on life as if she wanted to shake free a certain level of support for the Ten/Jared thing that was going on. She really didn't need to do that.

A simple, "Love is love," from me, and she nodded approvingly.

I shook Jared's hand and attempted a smile, which I hoped encompassed how I felt about him dating a dude, and how it was cool, and I accepted and supported it.

Likely, though, given the cold that was rattling my bones, it came out more of a grimace, because his eyebrows raised in question.

"It's all a bit much at first, new team and all," Jared said, and released his hold on my hand. He was giving me an out; offering me the chance to explain the half smile.

Best foot forward and all.

"Happy for you and Ten, Coach," I said, then blustered ahead to qualify the statement. "I like Tennant, he's a good kid." Shit. Had calling him "kid" drawn attention to the age difference between Coach Madsen and Tennant? Not that it was that bad, but… "I mean a good forward, good for the team."

At that, Coach smiled. "Thank you." He had a clipboard in his hand and a gaggle of kids standing behind him, all peering around him and staring up at me.

"Who's he?" someone faux-whispered, a young boy, no more than nine. This was clearly some kind of Railers outreach visit, or a school thing, or something like that. I put on my game face.

"Hi guys," I said, and stepped to one side so they could all see me. "Erik Gunnarsson, right wing."

There was a moment's hesitation, and then all hell broke loose—questions, comments, congratulations…a couple of the kids had even heard of me. Coach Madsen had to kind of corral them into a cohesive group, and you could tell he took the word "coach" to heart, because one word, and like a throng of ducklings they followed him away.

"Down here," Emma said, and continued to talk as we walked down the long corridor toward the elevators. "The Railers do a lot of outreach in the community, with schools. We have a newly formed sled team, work with several local charities, and have fundraising nights that you'll be expected to attend."

"Cool," I said, for want of something else to say. We'd had charity events in the San Diego Admirals, only they hadn't been quite as fancy as what I imagined an NHL team set up, like casino nights and puppy adoptions. Being a player wasn't just about the playing; the charity side, the outreach, they were all vital parts of my life. Back in Sweden as a kid, in my first team, I'd been in charge of fundraising. My gran had always said I could raise money just by using my dimples and curls.

Gran was obviously biased, but she'd been right that I *had* raised a lot of money.

And believe me, I have always known how to use my dimples and curls.

Emma called the elevator, and we waited in the cold corridor, me pulling down the sleeves of my worn Admirals jersey and her sinking deeper into her furry-hooded coat.

"We have a press release for tomorrow," she said. "Our social media consultant will want to schedule a meeting with you and suggested we drop by after the tour. That will be Layton Foxx, and I'll introduce you to him after you've got your bearings post-skate."

"Sure." I filed away the name. I'd seen the press conference for the guys on the team who were doing the horizontal, but the man who'd orchestrated how it all happened wasn't someone I knew.

The elevator arrived, and I gestured for Emma to go in first. She smiled at me, although to be fair I could see very little of her face under the fur of her hood. I smiled back and moved to the opposite side of the car. Hands off. No touching. Stay professional. Don't act available.

All wise words from my gran, my agent, and my best

friend Lars. They were the ones helping me pick up the pieces of my life—of being a husband, a father, and of a summer that had changed my life.

"This way," Emma said, and I followed her out into another corridor. I was seriously going to get lost. Everything was different on this floor. The walls were devoid of posters about the team and instead adorned with printouts of inspirational hockey quotes. The intensity of them grew as we moved closer to the dressing area. Seemed like someone on this team believed in the power of positive thought. Just as we were being told in stark black capitals that the Railers were winners, we reached double doors, and she stopped again. This time the Gunnarsson grace and control of my body played its part well, and I managed to stop in time.

"Your key card will get you into the changing room, and then into the locker room, so you need to have that on you at all times. Otherwise you'll find yourself locked in the corridor with no way in."

"Key card. Got it."

"Try it now."

I tugged at the card on the lanyard and waved it, as instructed, over the panel.

Ninety-five percent of me desperately hoped it didn't work. The same percentage that really wanted to have been picked up by an NHL team that wasn't the Railers. Any team. Even a shitty one that regularly beat my beloved New York Rangers.

Just my luck, it worked, and suddenly I was out of my comfort zone. In there was a team waiting for a new right wing; someone who could shore up their fourth line after they'd lost veteran Marc Gauthier to a long-term lower-body injury.

In there were skaters I knew well: Tennant Rowe, Adler

Lockhart, Jens Hedlund, Dieter Lehmann, Lee Addison, fellow Swede Arvid Ulfsson, and the captain Connor Hurleigh, to name but a few. Hell, Anatoly 'Toly' Sokolov was in there, and he was a personal hero of mine, not to mention my potential fellow winger on the fourth line.

"Are you okay?" Emma asked. "I know it can be over-whelming."

"I'm not overwhelmed. I'm excited," I reassured her.

I'm desperate to get on the ice for the Railers all while avoiding a big Russian.

"I'm just cold," I added, because she was probably reacting to my pale face or my shivering and taking it as nerves.

I wasn't nervous about the hockey or the players; that was my job, and I could do my job.

There was only one thing that was causing the butter-flies in my chest and the nausea that threatened.

Terror at coming face to face with Stanislav Lyamin. Stan, the man I'd loved and then thrown away last year. One conditioning camp, one long summer, and one affair I would never forget. I'd fallen in love, with the big goalie who spoke no English except for what he'd picked up in popular culture. We'd fallen for each other without much in the way of talking. Who does that kind of thing?

And Stan? He was the starting goalie for the Harris-burg Railers, and he was in that room.

"*Det blir som det blir,*" I murmured. "Whatever will be, will be."

Stan will ignore me, or hit me, or look at me with those tragically beautiful gray eyes.

"Sorry?"

"Superstition," I said quickly. People expected hockey players to do some weird things for good luck, and she nodded that she understood. The locker room door was also locked, accessed with the card, and after waving the card at the reader, we were in.

Noise died. What had been a cacophony of shouts, laughter and talking when I pushed the door open stopped dead. There was me thinking I could walk in to maybe a small group of the team, a subset of the entire team, maybe meet them a few at a time. But no, I wasn't going to be so lucky.

Everyone was in there, and one by one they acknowledged me with a handshake if they were close enough, or a welcoming nod if not.

Captain Connor Hurleigh crossed to me, shook my hand. "Welcome to the Railers," he said.

I have mad respect for Connor. Coming in as the captain of an expansion team is a challenge, and one that he'd managed, getting the new team to the playoffs last year. I had so much to say to him, so many questions, but all I could do was look for the one person who I couldn't immediately see in the room. Stan.

"Sorry about the lack of heating back here," Connor continued. "They said it would be fixed by three. You ready for this?"

I was half listening. Stan was seriously nowhere to be seen. And really, you couldn't miss the six-four giant mountain of a man, particularly in his goalie gear. His size had been one of the things that had attracted me. I'm not small, but I top out at six feet and carry thirty pounds less than he does. When we'd met in Sweden, all I'd been able to think had been that he was gorgeous, and sexy, and I wanted him.

So I'd worked harder on chasing Stan than I had on my conditioning.

I'd had Stan in my bed, and my heart, for the whole camp. I'd fallen in love, and then I'd been a coward. Or a hero? Who knew what I'd been; all that remained was that I'd thrown him away.

"Okay, then, let's get you suited up," Connor said, and his words pulled me back. Had I been standing there like an idiot? He didn't seem pissed at me, so maybe I hadn't fucked up on my first morning there. "Your stuff is in the stall. We put you with Toly."

Anatoly "Toly" Sokolov, fellow winger and future friend, I hoped, had a welcoming smile on his face, and talked to me the entire time I stripped and changed, pulling on the practice jersey of my new team. Practice jerseys were black and white, but the logo of a train was on all of them. Mine was black, the same as Toly's, and he fist-bumped me when I finished lacing my skates, thoughtfully available ready for me in my stall.

Stan was probably out on the ice. I could picture him now, graceful despite his size and his equipment. He'd be in net, maybe working on his stretches, or his blocker side, which he always complained was weaker than glove side. He'd be concentrating hard, and he wouldn't even notice I was there.

What was I to the big Russian anyway? A holiday fling? He'd walked away from me just as hard as I'd walked away from him. He understood we couldn't be together. He had a life that fit his NHL dreams.

I'd married Freja because it had been the right thing to do; we had a baby together. Even post break-up, my family thought I was managing wonderfully with my color-coded schedules and my nanny, but who was I kidding? My life wasn't together. My life was actually all kinds of messed up, and the fear of facing Stan for the first time since last summer wasn't helping at all.

I had a soon-to-be-official ex-wife, a new baby that I was the primary carer for, a nanny who saved my life on a daily basis, extensive debt, an empty rented apartment that needed filling, and a shark of a lawyer on speed-dial.

Today, here in this place, I had a Russian I needed to face.

I hit the ice, the smooth glide of skates on the cold stuff enough to snap me out of my misery as I pushed into lazy circles. Still no sign of Stan, and the backup goalie was out, leaning on his net and shooting the breeze with one of the coaches.

There was some joking, stretches, horsing around, and I began to take note of the rink, and the seating, and the huge jumbotron above my head.

Then the air shifted, or there was a noise, or I felt something. I don't know what it was exactly, but I knew *he* was there. I was still attuned to him, like he'd never left my heart or head at all. I just knew.

Connor patted my arm. "And this is Stan, our starting goalie."

TWO

Stan

There are many people I would have rather seen standing on the ice of my practice arena than Erik. For example my beloved sister, Galina, my sainted mother, Arina, my cat, Lucy, or my new gay American heartthrob, Zachary Quinto.

Zachary would be wearing only a smile even though it's cold on the ice.

But no, none of them were standing in front of me wearing a Railers sweater and curls. *Those damn golden curls.* They'd always tempted me beyond sense. As had his mouth. And the way he would tilt his head when he was trying to understand me out of bed. In bed? There was no language barrier. Our bodies had always been tuned to each other like radio waves to a satellite dish.

Even now, I felt the low hum of his presence in my veins. I had feared this moment would come. From the first time I'd heard his name mentioned as being a new member of the Rush, our AHL feeder team, I'd known he would eventually stand in front of me, tipping his head, with his curls, his eyes and his mouth.

Connor was looking at me as if he expected something from me. Ah yes, words. He wanted me to say something. How did "go fuck a donkey" translate into English?

"We are known to each other."

I skated to my net, mask perched on my head, and tried to focus. The humming in my blood was unsettling. Closing my eyes, I let the blue ice under my skates talk to me. Opening myself up to the sounds of hockey, the stress of seeing Erik again lessened. I whispered to the pipes as I tapped them. Asked them in Russian if they were going to be my friends during this practice.

"Uh, hey, I know this is a strict breach of protocol and all...but is there a problem between you and Gunner?"

I glanced to the left. Tennant stood there, geared up, his stick casually resting across his shoulders. So Erik now had his American hockey nickname. Why didn't I have a new American hockey nickname? Pah. I was being petty. It tasted bad on my tongue.

"Gunner is okay person from time back in space." Was that right? English was hard to speak. It made no sense. How could there be three ways to spell one word? Russian was simple. Strong. Pure. A language of passion and spirit. American was whiney and tied my brain into knots. No, that was not true. American was a wonderful language. It was me who was whiney and unhappy. "Time back. In the back of time. Is bad time to talk. Go away."

I waved my stick at him.

"Okay, yeah, sorry. Didn't mean to mess up your mojo, big man."

My best friend skated away, looking like a whipped dog. When he returned to the others, he shrugged, then they talked. About me. I knew it was about me. I was being stupid and making my friends confused. Truly, they couldn't be more confused than I was. On one hand, I hated Erik for using me, but I had used him too, a bit. More than a bit. But last summer in Helsinki had been meant to only be for sex, slaking the need. We had been the only two men who liked men among forty or so others. And he had been so handsome and smiled so prettily when I would wink at him secretly. Ugh. My pipes were not talking to me. They were angry that I was ignoring them.

"I am done with him in my head now. Only you." I ran my gloved hand over the icy steel.

When I turned to face center ice a moment later, every Railer was staring at me. But the only gaze that burned into my soul was Erik's.

"I am make good now with pipes. We may play." I reached up and flipped my mask down.

"So let it be written…" Adler Lockhart said, and many laughed. I didn't know what that meant. There was so much said around me that I didn't understand. I felt like the foreigner that I was all the time. Sometimes I wanted to just go home to my mother, but that wouldn't be safe. Russia was not a good place for a gay man. Mama knew that and never asked for me to come back home to visit. She and my baby sister were the only ones who knew. And Erik, of course. Keeping the secret had kept me safe, perhaps even alive, until I could leave Mother Russia.

"Stan, are you feeling okay?"

My gaze flew to Alain Gagnon, our goalie coach, who had skated up on my left unseen. So bad. That was so bad. My concentration was gone today. I blamed Erik and his curls.

"Yes, fine. Fit as fiddle." I grinned and tapped my chest with my blocker. "Someone shoot puck at me!"

They all stared at me like idiots. I looked at Alain. He was not a handsome man, but he knew goaltending. He wore two diamond-studded Cup rings. How many did I wear? None. That was because I let things like Erik's bouncy blond ringlets make my pipes stop talking.

"You do know that if you need to talk to me about anything, I'm right down the hall from the dressing room."

"Yes, I know. I am good. Strong in head."

He nodded. I nodded.

"Shoot pucks at me!" I bellowed.

The squads hurried to comply. Angry Russians seemed to intimidate them for some reason. Blocking shots would be good for me. Alain skated off after giving me a funny look.

The first shot came from Tennant. It hit me dead center of my black practice jersey, right in the train on my chest. I drew in a long breath through my nose, exhaled, and let the puck drop to the ice. It got kicked away. Another shot came at me from the left, another soft one. Warm-up shots. Each man took several at me, even Erik. His snap shot had improved since we'd been on the ice together last. A flash of my glove up, and I had the blistering shot neatly caught.

And then it started again, over and over, the shots growing faster, harder, more accurately aimed. Sweat ran down my neck, into my eyes, down my back. It was good sweat, though, cleansing sweat. The sweat of hard work. That was a sweat any poor Russian boy was familiar with.

Now that I was in my head, the pipes felt warmer to me. Happy to have me near. They caught two slap shots and sang out in joy. Such good pipes. They were truly a goalie's best friend.

Coach Benning gave us a talk after scrimmage had ended. I was seated alone, my back to the other men, hoping I could undress and shower without seeing Erik again. It was a bad situation there in the dressing room.

"Tomorrow night we're hosting Boston. I want you all

to have your skates sharp and your heads on straight. We're in a three-way tie for first in our division. Every game counts. Every point is important. The battle for bragging rights for Pennsylvania is on the line."

Everyone mumbled in agreement. Philadelphia, Pittsburgh, and Harrisburg were all log-jammed at the top of the Eastern Division. With about a third of the season behind us, now was the time to make sure we did not slip.

"Tomorrow's skate is optional. I want you all rested and mentally sharp. Boston will not lie down for us. They're big, tough, and hungry. They want to stay on top in the Atlantic Division as badly as we want to stay on top in the Eastern. So go home, sleep, eat, meditate, do whatever it is that gets your head into the space where we need it to be."

Coach Benning walked out then. The dressing room got loud. Men laughed and talked. Someone turned on some music. Dieter yelled at Adler about hairbands. Dirty socks flew overhead. I paid it all little mind. I needed to get showered, leave, and go home to Lucy. Maybe watch TV and plan more for my party for New Year's. My sister was coming. She had never seen my home in Harrisburg. She was so excited to finally see America. My mother also had been invited, but her fear of flying kept her grounded in Leskovo, the dying little farming town I had grown up in. I invited her weekly, it seemed, and she always refused.

If only I could go back and sit beside her on the plane, hold her hand, but she would not let me. She feared my secret being discovered just as deeply as she did getting onto a plane.

"Hey, we're all going to get together at our place for some Pokémon training. You want to come?" Tennant sat down beside me. He had just left the showers and had a towel around his lean waist. Water ran from his hair down his nose.

"No, thank you. I have food-planning for party."

My friend slapped my sweaty shoulder. "Okay, cool. I hope you have those cheese pancake things like you had last year. Those were freaking incredible!"

"*Syrniki*. Yes. I have those coming with catering."

"You rock." Tennant bumped the side of my fist with his, then leaped to his bare feet and ambled off to talk with Arvy and Dieter.

My gaze moved over the room and landed on Erik. Undressing, his back to us, showing me and the world his ass. It was still as tight and high as I recalled. Try as I might, I couldn't look away from his backside. Skate dangling from my hand by its laces, the tidal wave of memories from our summer together crashed over me, pulling me out to sea in a salty, frothy wash of remembered passion.

Erik spread out over the bed in my tiny room in the training center, one hand gripping the headboard tightly and the other over his mouth to mute his cries of pleasure. I was between his spread legs, his beautiful prick in my mouth, working his tight ass with three fingers. His body was slick with sweat, as the air conditioning in my room was weak. Sitting in Harrisburg, I could still smell him. That tangy aroma of man, sweat, sex, and cucumber-melon soap filled my nose even now. I could hear the head-board creaking as he pulled strongly on it each time my fingers stroked his prostate. And if I closed my eyes, I could taste him. Musky and male on my tongue as he came, coating my throat. He thrashed madly, pumping deeply, making me gag and groan. I took myself in hand then, with the zest of him thick on my tongue, and stroked myself hard and fast until my palm was slick with my release.

I dreamily tasted my lips and found them dry and lacking the erotic flavor of Erik Gunnarsson that I'd become so addicted to last summer. Now I felt battered and bruised, as if that wave of hot lust had beaten me against the rocky shore of reality. When I opened my eyes, Erik's gaze met mine. I shifted uncomfortably, my hard cock unhappy over the cramped conditions of the two cups pressing against it.

His eyes were such a stunning shade of green, and the undercurrent of emotion and want began to tug on me yet again. Just a taste, maybe...for old time's sake, as they say. One hot, hard purging of any lingering tenderness. In the skate-sharpening room maybe. Up against the wall... Ugh! This situation was...was...

"*Pizdets*," I muttered, my gaze flying from Erik to the water cooler.

"What is fucked up?" Toly asked while walking behind me to the showers.

"What is not?" I grunted, and threw my skate into my cubicle. I spoke to no one else as I stripped and showered. My friends tried talking to me while I was dressing, but I remained inside myself, eager to put distance between Erik and my upset.

"Stan, where are you going?" Toly shouted at my back as I stalked from the dressing room, winter coat on my back, large lapels up to shield my ears from the wind and cold. "Stanislav, you rode in with me!"

I bulled through the door, ignoring Peter, the nice security man who stood guard by the players' entrance. Peter called out something to me as the door slammed shut but I didn't answer. Now I felt bad. This wasn't me. I was always nice to people because mostly I liked them all.

I stepped out into the weather, turned from the players' cars, and headed to the street out of the back entrance. Fans didn't know I did this otherwise they might have been waiting and one day they'd figure it out, but that day wasn't this one.

Then I stood huddled up with several other people, waiting for a bus. No fan would assume the goalie for the Railers would be taking a bus and that was working for me right now.

No one huddled here talked to anyone. Usually people smiled or nodded at me because I stood out a bit. Today, they looked up at me then glanced away. My angry face must be scaring them. I didn't see anyone pull out a phone and take photos though; people here seemed to respect my privacy.

Large, flat flakes blew around the bus shelter, adding fluffy inches to the already heavy amount of snow on the ground.

The cold didn't bother me too much. When the bus pulled up, I admit to being glad to see it, though. The warm air flowed out of the open door. I allowed an old woman to enter before me, then I climbed into the city bus, taking a seat by a window.

It would take several buses and a few changeovers to reach home, but that was good. It would give me time to clear my head. A man behind me coughed wetly. Hopefully I'd not catch the flu that was going around. Burrowing into my coat, I pulled out my phone and found a music app that Tennant had shown me how to work. Since I read little to no English, everything in America was a struggle for me. Driving, for instance. I was not yet licensed in Pennsylvania but was studying the drivers' manual hard. The state issued them in Russian, and the test was given in several languages, Russian being one of them. Anatoly had helped me find all this information on a Russian website the state had set up. That was kind of the people who ran Pennsylvania. I know many people say that we should not get benefits if we do not speak English, but truly, it is a hard language, and we who come here are trying hard.

In the spring I would be ready, I felt, to take the drivers' test. That would make me even more American. That was my goal. To become an American citizen and bring my mother and sister over to live with me. There was little in Russia for a man like me. But here in America, there were roads lined with yellow bricks. No. Was that right? Gold bricks, maybe.

I pulled out my phone and looked up yellow bricks. They were not in America but in Oz. I liked that movie. I liked so much about America, the hard language aside. The food was good, the movies filled with action and sex, and the music was uniquely American.

The bus rolled along, stopping to let people on and off. I found my earbuds and slid them in, content to bounce along until I had to catch another bus for the final ride out to Hershey. My playlists were long and had funny names. Tennant had told me to give them funny names as he did our groups chats on the computer. Those I also had trouble reading, but the pictures and gifs were funny.

This one that was playing now was my favorite. I had named it "King of Las Vegas and World", because Elvis was that. I loved him so much. Hearing him sing made me happy, and happy was what I needed now. Happy would always win out over unhappy. So I listened to Elvis singing, working on trying to memorize the lyrics because Elvis spoke good English. It was very hip and cool English too. His movies were hip and cool, just like him.

It took me over an hour to get from the arena to my

neighborhood. The ride with Anatoly usually took half that, but I had needed the time alone. Walking along the well-groomed streets, I was peaceful inside now. My house was waiting for me, tucked back among some big trees. The siding was gray and the shutters black. It was a big house. Five bedrooms and three bathrooms. Plenty of room for my sister and mother to settle in. I might have gone wild when I chose it, since I was a bachelor, but maybe…someday…I'd have a husband and enough children to fill all those bedrooms. That was also my dream. American citizen, Stanley Cup champion, beloved husband and father, and my mother and sister there to enjoy all my success and spoil the children.

As I stepped inside my massive house, there was no husband or child to greet me. I stamped the snow from my shoes, tossed my keys and phone to the table in the foyer, and called out for my cat.

"Lucy, I am home," I shouted, and my sweet kitty ran down the stairs, meowing loudly. I picked up the long-haired brown cat and draped her over my shoulder. She purred and began pulling threads out of my suit jacket as she kneaded. "Silly cat. Let's eat and watch 'Viva Las Vegas' again."

Elvis and Ann-Margaret. Yes. They would be far less confusing than thinking about Erik and how his hard body fit so perfectly next to mine.

THREE

Erik

———————

When a coach tells you that a skate is optional that doesn't apply equally to every member of the team. Arvy was there working on his accuracy, and then there was me, and Toly, and the last man in our line, Martin "Charlie" Brown. We would be working together tonight against Boston, and today was all about getting a feel for each other. We'd practiced yesterday, but this was more concerning skating in a simple cohesive line and passing the puck.

I'd never played with Toly before, and to be honest I was still overwhelmed that I got to play on the same line as him at all.

Charlie, on the other hand, had attended a lot of the same intense training and conditioning schools as I had in summer breaks, including the fateful one where Stan and I had *happened*.

Please don't Charlie talk about last summer.

We skated in soft, flowing movements, getting our line in sync. Toly was slower, but his accuracy was spot on, Charlie was like a damn greyhound, and me? I managed to find a rhythm that was halfway between. I had to study my line, learn Charlie and Toly, the look of them, the way they reversed direction, how fast they were, how quickly they could pass, the moves they made, and had game tape keyed up that I could check out later.

"I want to see you a step ahead, Charlie," Coach Benning said as we huddled around him. "Toly, you're backing this up." He tapped the board that held an assortment of Xs and Os. "Use your speed, Charlie, get into position—and Gunner, I need you here, so that you can cover their D getting to Charlie and get that puck over the center line."

I listened to every word, even said my bit when asked if I had questions, and then Charlie and Toly called it a day, which left me alone on the ice. There'd been no sign of Stan today, and why would there be? He was a starting goalie who was likely at home doing some of those incredibly impressive stretches that had made my mouth water every time I'd seen them.

If you haven't made love with a stretchy-bendy goalie, then you haven't lived.

A second person joined me in lazy circles. Arvid "Arvy" Ulfsson was not only a fellow Swede, but he'd lived only a few towns over from Ornskoldsvik, which is where I grew up. Everyone in and around O-vik plays hockey, like hockey town Sweden. He knew the beautiful summers and the dark, cold winters on icy lakes as well as I did.

"*Det var länge sedan vi sågs sist,*" he said as we fell into a smooth set of figure eights, crossing in the center of the rink. *Long time no see.*

We were around the same age, but he'd been drafted and actually played NHL hockey straight from his second year. The six-foot defenseman was one of these eternally happy guys, the one on the bench who kept spirits high even if you were losing so badly you just wanted to go and hide in the locker room. I liked him, and hell, he spoke Swedish. Of course, we both spoke excellent English—in Swedish schools it's a pre-requisite, along with a love of hockey, it seems. But sometimes you just want to talk in your own language and know that it's just the two of you who understand.

"How are you?" I asked, the familiar vowels and syllables of Swedish relaxing me. I needed that after spending the first part of the session waiting for Charlie to ask me about *that summer* and to have to field questions like, "Didn't you and Stan get super close?"

"Doing good." Arvy switched so he was skating backward, shadowing me, feinting left then right, turning back, icing to a stop and then skating at speed away from me. This was his role—defending, following their forwards whatever they did. I gave nothing away, but tried a few moves and managed to shake him off once. By the time we were finished, we were laughing, leaning on the wood, shooting the breeze about home and family and people we knew.

Of course he would know about Freja, and the fact that we'd married, and that we'd had a baby. The Swedish skaters had a network of gossip, and I knew it must have come up.

"Sorry to hear about you and Freja," he said, lifting his water bottle and squirting a healthy mouthful. "Must be hard."

"It's okay," I reassured him, "it was a mutual thing."

Arvy nodded. "And you have a baby, I heard? A little one."

"Noah. He's nearly nine months now. He's living with me." I gave him the look I gave everyone, daring him to ask why he wasn't with his mom. Arvy didn't even go there; clearly my expression of warning was enough.

Noah and I were fine on our own, happier than if I'd stayed with Freja just because it was expected. We had our nanny, Amy, and the three of us rattling around in my empty apartment were exactly right and as it should be.

"I can't believe you're a dad," Arvy said with a grin. "Changing diapers, burping the little one, getting up in the night…"

"This is why I have a nanny."

I let him think I did nothing, but in all honesty, sitting up with Noah in the early hours of the morning, holding him, finding my Zen space with him curled on my chest, was my idea of heaven. He had the same curls as me— Freja called it his curse, but she was always looking for things that made Noah more mine and less hers, so I ignored what she said. Noah also had my green eyes, although his had tiny amber flecks. I had photos on my phone, but I wasn't ready to let anyone in to see those yet.

Not even a man I'd known back home.

We parted with smiles and a promise to get together soon, and that was it—my morning there was done.

Most players take naps in the afternoon. I took a nap if Noah let me, which today he did. Curled up next to me, his arms flung out, he slept the sleep of the innocent. Getting to sleep myself was a slow process, so I honestly had no idea if the nap had done any good at all. Still, when I woke I felt ready to get back to the rink.

After I'd laid on the sofa and cuddled Noah a bit longer while Amy went shopping.

"So I met Stan again," I began to explain to Noah, who blew tiny bubbles from his mouth as he drank his milk. I'd talked about Stan before to Noah—how we'd met, how I'd fallen so hard, but how I'd made a decision that was best for all of us. "He's so big, and if he was holding you…"

A sudden image of Stan holding Noah struck me front and center. Stan was a gentle giant when he wasn't either icily in control or angry in goal, and Noah would look up at him and smile and…

I had to stop that.

"So anyway, the game Daddy plays, hockey, he plays it too."

I rocked Noah to sleep after playing with him a little; he was beginning to cruise the furniture in a stumbling fashion, and it fascinated me. Everything about Noah fascinated me, from the golden curls on his head to his big green eyes, and the way he seemed to smile with his entire body. I picked up my cell and took a few selfie kind of shots of Noah and emailed them to myself. One day I needed to actually print some of these photos and put them up on the wall. Not the walls of this place, but my real place when I finally moved to it.

I regretted not taking the Railers up on the offer of a temporary place, but they talked as if it was this rookie bachelor hub, and hell, I had a baby, and a nanny.

In those moments when I was really honest with myself, though, I knew it was my stubborn need to prove I could do this baby-daddy thing on my own that meant I was now in this old building that smelled faintly of cat pee and boiled cabbage.

Never let it be said that I have any sense at all.

"I'm going to send a picture to your momma," I whispered to a sleeping Noah, and opened an app, adding the photo and sending it to her. I didn't expect a reply; I never did. But I knew she was overseas; one thing she did do was share her calendar with me in case of emergency.

Although what that meant, I didn't know. I guessed if

Noah needed a blood transfusion or bone marrow, because hell, that was the only way his mom would go anywhere near him. Flicking through Google hits on her name, I found a disturbing trend of her putting herself in more danger with each assignment. Afghanistan was the latest hit—three months, front line, right in the camera, ducking explosions, and looking gorgeous at the same time.

The woman I'd slept with, twice, before I met Stan, was stunning. Long blonde hair, blue eyes, and a beautiful smile that her son had inherited. We'd met at a local hero's awards show, both giving away prizes to young adults who had faced danger and won. She didn't look quite so picture perfect in the latest photo, hair scraped back under a helmet, her fatigues blending in with the pile of stones behind her, but she looked alive and vital. She loved being a journalist, wanted nothing more than to stand at the very front of what was terrifying or dangerous, and make the world sit up and take notice.

I'd been drawn to that danger, fucking her in the bathroom at the awards, then again against a wall in her room.

Twice, and on one of those two times Noah had been conceived.

But Noah and me? We didn't have Freja anymore. No one had her; she belonged to a different world than us.

"She'll always love you," I half-lied. I actually wasn't entirely sure how she felt about Noah, only that I'd paid her to let me have him, something he would never know about.

Call it stupidity, call it the result of having shitty parents, call it my own stubborn nature, but we'd created life, and that was important to me.

A small part of me actually blamed Stan. I slept with Freja before that fateful summer camp. I didn't know Freja was pregnant until *after* that time with Stan.

Stan had shown me how easy it was to love someone, how a connection could be made, and suddenly my somewhat shallow life had begun to mean more. So when Freja contacted me and explained what had happened, that was when I'd made the decision.

Have the baby, please.

She'd already been twelve weeks, hadn't even realized, had thought it was stomach flu, or something she'd picked up in her time in Honduras.

She'd told me didn't want the baby, that she was addicted to being scared, that she needed the passion of journalism, or crossing time zones and explaining disaster and pain for public consumption.

Who was I to argue? I wanted…*needed* hockey. It was my life.

Or it had been my life.

What she didn't realize was that the deep-seated fears and the overwhelming love that you have for a child are enough adrenaline to get any parent through the day.

My cell vibrated, and it was her.

He looks well. How are you?

I thought carefully about my reply. Her question wasn't about how Noah was, but to me there was no longer just-Erik, we were now Erik/Noah, and so my reply was a little broader.

We're doing fine. Saw you'd been in A.

A break, and I imagined her in a tent in the middle of nowhere, which was where she spent most of her life.

A was bad. Home in New Year.

I only had one thing to say that. No, scratch that, two.

Stay safe. Come visit if you like.

And clearly, she had two things to say to me.

Staying safe. I don't think I will visit.

I didn't hate her for it. I wondered if one day Noah

would. If I had to make a choice between Noah and hockey, between Noah and the icy dreams of winning a championship, I would choose Noah every time.

Every. Single. Time.

When it came time for me to leave, Amy took him from me, wished me luck at the game, and mentioned that furniture would be good. She said that every day. I should just give her my credit card, but to be honest, until money funneled to me from the Railers, I was seriously fucked. I mumbled something in return—a vague grunt that could be taken to mean anything—and she shook her head and went into the kitchen.

She was used to me now.

Every penny I had, bar some that I'd kept back to live on, had gone. I had a six hundred-thousand-dollar contract and nothing to show for it apart from a rented roof over my head, enough money to pay for Amy, and my shitty car. At least I had Noah with me; that was what mattered.

The rest of my money? Well, let's say it had taken that much to get lawyers to draw up papers, to divorce Freja and invest money in her career. I'd had paperwork signed and notarized, she'd waived her rights, Noah was mine, and in less than three months we would have a final divorce. Money consumed my thoughts, though and I wondered if I should approach management for some kind of loan.

I was so lost in thoughts of balancing check books and wondering where was the best place to get furniture that I didn't see him.

Or feel him in that crazy sixth-sense way I'd had in Helsinki.

Not until I crashed straight into the one man I didn't want to talk to, or see again.

Stan caught me, and I stumbled before he hauled me close to keep me upright.

"Stupid," Stan said, making it sound less a word and more a curse. Then he pushed me away, not roughly, but definitely firmly.

Then we stood face to face, or at least my eyeline to his chin, and we didn't move.

"I have so much I want to say," I began. Why was I doing this? He wasn't interested in what I wanted to say. Not about the regrets, or the fact that I never should have left.

The last thing we'd said, or rather that I'd said for us both, was that the summer was done and our lives would move on.

"Not listen, stupid," Stan said, and crossed his arms over his wide chest. He stared down at me with an unforgiving frown and tension radiating from every pore of him. The way he spoke, the stilted cute words, was enough to have me thinking back to that summer, in one rush of heat and sex and need.

"I want to say something. Anything. Sorry, maybe?"

He looked at me suspiciously. "Sorry?" he asked after a small pause.

"For making decisions for both of us, for the summer, for everything."

"Hmmm," he said, then uncrossed his arms. I saw he had a tattoo—something yellow, but I couldn't make it out. He'd never had a tattoo before, and I knew, because I'd kissed, licked, and bitten my way over every inch of him.

"Hmmm?" I prompted, because he seemed to be formulating a response somewhere along the line. Probably he had the words in Russian, and was now parsing them into coherent English.

"One day to meet wife and baby," he said. Then he

subsided, like that simple sentence had stolen all his energy. Jeez, it had been easier when he'd used television commercials to form his sentences.

Wait? My wife? My baby? Is he talking about Noah? He knows about Noah? Of course he does; anyone with an Instagram account knows about my marriage.

How must it have looked? The photos out there of me marrying a pregnant Freja must have had him thinking only one thing, that I'd cheated on her with him, when that wasn't true. So maybe that was what I needed to explain, about how she'd been a one night-stand, and that we'd conceived Noah, and that to a man like me marriage had been the only option.

I blinked. I know I did. I know I was looking at him, and my mouth was probably open. Was he saying now that he wanted to meet Noah? Or that he didn't? How did I explain that I didn't have a wife anymore, that she'd left me just as I'd left him? How did I explain that she was a wife in name only, that she was Noah's mom but nothing more?

"Baby and wife," he repeated.

"For you?" I asked, really confused.

"Team." He waved a hand. "Bring here baby, for luck."

Oh. He meant the team. Not him. Not Stan.

I guessed that was what I should have expected. Sadness curled inside me, and I knew I should explain, say something. Anything.

"I want to tell you the truth—"

"*Nyet. Ya vse znayu.* Know it."

"But you can't know, I'm nearly divorced and—"

"*Nyet.*"

"When I was with you, it was only you. I promise that, Stan."

He stared at me, then he reached for my head and

carded one hand through my hair, tugging gently as his fingers caught in the curls.

"Like gold," he murmured, and I swayed toward him, half erect at the sound of the deep, rumbling voice. Then he yanked his hand free, cursed loudly, and stalked past me in the corridor.

The sadness and disquiet settled in for the evening, even right up to the coach's speech at the beginning of the game.

"Ten, keep your eye on your brother, I want to know if you see anything, okay?"

I knew Ten's brother was the captain of the Boston team. It always helped to have some insider knowledge, but equally they would be saying the same for Ten, keeping an eye on our star player.

"On it, Coach," Ten agreed, and fist-bumped Arvy.

Stan sat very quiet in his corner, and I recollected that he'd done that in Helsinki. He would often sit quietly, eyes closed, humming softly. The memories flooded me again, and there was that familiar sadness laced with regret.

Maybe I should bring Noah in one day. Maybe if Stan saw us together, saw the unconditional love I was capable of giving... Then maybe Stan might like me again, and then I could explain how I'd packed to go back to him the night my life changed forever.

That was all I wanted.

The game was hard; you can't go up against an elite team like Boston and not feel it in every aching muscle. We were only just beginning the third period, one goal down, and Ten skated as if he was on fire. He was everywhere and nowhere, and the Boston defense was losing sight of him more often than not. Eight shots on goal from him so far, and one of them had to go in. Surely.

Stan was a wall for us. He'd only let in two goals, one

of them questionable as to whether there had been goal-tender interference. Arvy certainly let the Boston D know he was unhappy with a nice left hook. We killed that power play, but only because Stan stood on his damn head to block the puck.

Five minutes left in the game, and one of the Boston Ds was given a penalty for hooking, abruptly we were on a power play. Somehow, in the blink of an eye, with magic that left the bench in silence, Ten was there, and this time the puck went right past their goalie and the score was tied.

Everyone shouted for Ten, and when he skated past the bench, touching gloves, he wore a wide grin.

But I wasn't looking at Ten. I was looking way past him, at the way Stan leaned on his pipes, at the grin I could make out from here.

I might have decided that things had ended, but clearly my brain hadn't informed my libido, or more importantly, my heart.

FOUR

Stan

"*Ya lyublyu tebya.*" Words of affection and adoration. *I love you.* And I did. And they loved me. Tonight, my pipes had been loving friends, catching three Boston shots. I rubbed the cold metal pipe with my catcher as the Railers fans chanted and stamped their feet. "*Lyubite menya nemnogo dol'she,*" I added, asking them to love me just a bit longer. I turned from my net and glanced at the clock. Only two minutes left. Something pulled at me, making me look at the Railers bench. At Erik.

Anger bubbled up inside my chest. Pain, too. So much pain, fresh, as if he'd just walked out on me yesterday. The ache in my chest felt like bad heartburn, or when one has drunk too much vodka and vomits it back up. That was what I felt looking at my ex-lover, that burning fire racing up my throat. Why had I been so stupid as to fall for him so quickly? Why did I give my heart so easily? Lust had driven me to lure him to my bed. And he had been eager to come. *So* eager. And so willing. He had held me as if he cared. Whispered tender things. My Swedish was bad, his

Russian worse, but the emotions and feelings had spoken for us. But I'd thought he might stay with me, somehow, when camp ended. Although in all honesty it seemed stupid now to have had such romantic dreams. A gay Russian man did not flaunt his homosexuality by moving in with a pretty, blond Swedish man back home. It just wasn't done, especially out in the country where I had been raised. Yes, there were young people in the cities who were accepting, but not enough. Not nearly enough... Deep down, I think, I knew this, but still I dreamed. Of him, of a life with him, children, love. Here in America this dream could be real. Men could marry here in this wonderful country. They could adopt children, even! Even now the fantasy wanted to settle on my shoulders, but I shook it off like an unwanted embrace. I hated him. Yes. And that was how it would remain. How it must remain if I were to keep my heart.

I was so lost in the past drama that the shot from Brady Rowe hitting my shoulder startled me. I flopped my arm up and over my head, batting the puck away. Tennant's brother was like a wolfhound on the scent of its prey. Big, fierce, and determined, the eldest Rowe slid into my crease, his stick working around my skates. That made me mad. Him being in my blue ice and my being angry with Erik left me feeling dumb and unprofessional.

"Fuck off, stupid face!" I snarled at Brady, then shoved him. Hard. He went to his ass and I kicked the puck away from my net. Of course, the Railers who were on the ice skated into my net, as did the other Boston players. Pushing and shoving happened. Whistles blew. Players fell on top of Brady. The clock was stopped as men rolled around on the ice, trying to pull off sweaters and helmets while a TV timeout was called. I grabbed my water bottle and skated past the knot of players on the ice. Seeing

Brady pinned by Adler Lockhart's big body, I took my advantage and squirted him in the face with my drinking water.

He spat and cursed. I skated to my bench, smiling widely, knowing I'd probably get a fine, but it would be worth it. I could afford it. My contract gave me close to two million dollars a year. What was a few thousand lost in a fine?

"Fucking Aquaman right here!" Tennant shouted amid the peals of laughter. I grinned at my friend and let the players tousle my sodden hair. "I wish it had been me doing that to him!"

A trainer took my old water bottle and filled it with fresh, cold water—you fill the bottle but do not replace it because there is luck with my old bottle—while I took pats on the back from everyone but Erik. His gaze and mine tangled, though. He inclined his head. I did the same. Then I skated back to my crease with cold water and doused myself repeatedly while the penalty minutes were being assigned.

We ended up with ninety seconds of four-on-four. Brady Rowe had been assessed a goaltender interference call and Adler Lockhart had gotten a roughing penalty. Four-on-four was good for me; there was more room on the ice, and I could see plays developing that much faster. Not much happened until the final twenty seconds, when a rolling shot deflected off the skate of my ex...whatever he was. Erik was trying to defend the net, I knew that. It was what the coaches call a "freaky deflection" that I simply couldn't adjust quickly enough to stop. The puck slithered under my right leg pad a second before I could seal pad to ice. The red light flashed, and Boston celebrated right in my face.

"I'm sorry, Stan. I didn't even see the shot," Erik was

saying as I closed my eyes and looked heavenward, resting on my ass in my crease. I didn't have a response for him, so I just got to my feet and gave him my back. My pipes and I had a long talk in Russian. Erik had left the ice by the time I'd stopped explaining myself to my pipes, who had done all they could this night.

The loss stung a bit but, as always with sports, it was crucial not to dwell. Goalies especially can get mental blocks over a bad luck shot like that one that had bounced off Erik's skate. During the post-game interviews, I was asked how I felt about the bad goal by Gunner.

"Was not bad for him. Was bad for me. Was on me big bad."

The reporters nodded and moved on, gathering around Erik. Watching him trying to apologize to the city about that goal, I felt bad for him. A little bit.

After the press left, we showered. Not Erik and me, no, that was not happening ever again. I made sure he was out of the showers before I went in. When I was drying off in front of my cubicle, several players gathered around me.

"Hey, big guy," Tennant said. I gave him a look that made him smile awkwardly. "Glad to hear that you're cool with what happened out there." He jerked his dark head toward the ice.

"Is cool for papermen," I replied, and returned to organizing my kit layer by layer.

The gang of half-dressed players lingered. I flung my shoulder pads into my cubicle, lifted my gaze from my pads lying on their side, and glowered at the men assembled around me.

"Stan, we know there's some sort of past with you and Gunner. I mean, you'd have to be blind to miss the animosity," Connor was now saying in his best captain tone of voice. Tennant I could push off, also Adler, Arvy, Dieter, and the rest, but the captain? No. Him I listen to, because he is our leader. I began to speak. Connor lifted a hand. "I don't need to know what it is, but I do need to say that whatever it is needs to be handled. The tension is creeping into the locker room and affecting the team."

"I understand good," I replied. Connor lifted an eyebrow. "I do. I understand good." The words were jamming up inside my head. So many whirling thoughts and sentiments. Sorting the language was hard. "I'm not mad at Erik more."

"I'm not asking you to go over and kiss the man on the mouth or anything," Connor interjected. A flash of buried memory flared to life. Of me doing just that, capturing Erik's mouth as we tripped and stumbled into my hotel room, his hands pulling at my shirt, my fingers wound in all those golden curls. My body reacted with a rush of need that surged to my crotch. "Just try not to make it so obvious that you and him have issues."

"Truth," said Adler. "There are players that we all have trouble with, right? But for this team to *steam* onward to the playoffs, we can't let that dislike *derail* us." He grinned at me. "See what I did there? I went with the train motif because we're Railers and...yeah. Okay, I'm going to go shower now."

"Dude has got a point, Stan," Tennant chimed in as Connor continued to study me like a bug pinned to a board. "Harmony is important. Maybe you could just go shake the guy's hand or something?"

"I will do or something on morning time."

"Maybe you should do it now."

I threw a dark look at Connor Hurleigh. I did not like his captain talk right now. So I stood up and continued with the bad eyeballs.

"No time like the present," he added as I tried to stare

him down. Usually my size intimidated most, but not our captain. He folded his arms over his bare chest and tipped up his chin.

"Fine. I am shaking hands now." I stormed through the two men blocking me, nearly sending Tennant to his ass, and stalked up to Erik. I slapped his back. He grunted and whirled around to see who had struck him. I extended my hand. His beautiful green eyes darted from my face to my open palm. "All is groovy."

"Ah, okay. Thanks, Stan." He placed his hand in mine.

The other men in the room—hell, the room itself—seemed to be swallowed up by the universe. It was only Erik and me, skin on skin, eyes locked. Memories rode over me unbidden, like Cossack horsemen. The first time I saw him. Our bumbling attempts to communicate back when my English was not as peachy keen as it was now. His laughter, his smile, the way he tipped his head, the spark of desire in those emerald eyes, the feel of him under me, his body clamping down around me as he bucked and arched back for more of my cock.

I ripped my hand from his, my prick hard but thankfully well hidden behind my cups. I turned and walked back to my space.

"Is good now. Go leap off tall building in single bound."

Tennant snorted and clapped my back. Connor gave me a smile. Then they left me alone. I sat there, head down, waiting for my prick to soften and for Erik to leave. I waited until they were all gone. Only then did I go wash away the sweat. I dressed in silence, my thoughts and body confused about everything. Pete, the security man, stood at the player's exit. He was a handsome man. His tattooed arm was impressive and masculine.

"Sorry about that fluke. Happens, though, right?"

"Yes, flukes happen. I am off to see pussy now."

Pete laughed. "Yeah, I bet you are. Night, Stan."

I looked at him oddly, then stepped outside. It was so cold. Deep cold that goes into your bones like back home. I missed my mother then. Terribly so. Going home to my big empty house was depressing. Soon I would be twenty-eight, and had no one to go home to but Lucy.

"Yo, dude, about time, man! Come on." Tennant appeared in front of me. He grabbed me by the arm and tugged me to a fancy car that Coach Madsen owned. "Took you long enough."

"I am going home with bus," I argued when Ten opened the back door and waved at me to get in.

"No, we're taking you home. Now get in," Tennant said.

I planted my feet firmly in the few inches of new snow. "No, I am going home with bus."

"Stan, please get in. I'm too tired to sit here and listen to you two fight about this." Coach Madsen sighed wearily, his arms dangling over the steering wheel.

I got in, but only because he was a coach. Tennant dashed around and climbed into the front seat beside Coach Madsen.

"When are you going to go for your test?" Tennant asked as we made our way to Hershey. His upbeat bopper music was playing. It was bouncy but not as bouncy as "Good Luck Charm".

"Soon."

"Cool! You're going to rake in all the babes cruising through Hardscrabble." Tennant and Jared laughed. I didn't understand how I could drive through a board game. Americans spoke bizarrely at times. "Buy a convertible!"

41

"Those are hardly good cars to own when one lives where it snows," Coach Madsen said.

"They put heaters in them. You old men and your chilly feet."

"You weren't complaining about my chilly feet last night."

I stopped listening to them tossing couple banter back and forth. Instead I just grunted and nodded until I was out of the car and safely in my house. Then I let my coat slide off my arms, and the yearning for someone doubled. Lucy appeared then, purring and acting silly. I bent down and picked her up. She licked my nose with her rough tongue.

"You have breath like dead tuna," I told her, then walked through my house, looking at all the bedrooms and wondering if I would ever fill them. Could I ever find someone who would love me as I loved Erik? *Had* loved. I did not love him now. I hated him. Yes. "We hate him like moldy bread on sandwich after bite."

I paused in the doorway of my bedroom, Lucy draped around my neck like a sable stole, and thought on what I had said.

"We hate him like bite of sandwich with bread that is molding. Yes, that is much good English."

Lucy meowed in agreement. I reached up and removed the brown cat from my shoulders and dropped her onto the bed. It was eleven at night. I stripped off my suit and threw it into the hamper. Soon I would need to go to the dry cleaners to pick up my clean suits and drop off the dirty ones. I crawled into my bed, in nothing but my sexy boxer briefs that Tennant said all studs wear, and found Netflix on the plasma TV set attached to the wall. Lucy walked over my thighs, making toenail tracks until I removed her from my lap and told her to stay on her side of the bed.

"You have much room," I said while wagging a finger at her. She rubbed her cheek over my finger, then curled up on the spare pillow.

"Let us find something good to make us feel better about shit life," I said. Lucy twitched an ear in reply.

I found my list of good movies. So many Elvis. Some were explosion movies that Tennant or Adler had suggested. Lots of fire and guns while the actors walked away from them with *Cool Hand Luke* attitudes. I flipped through the collection of gay movies I had on a list, but so many of them ended sadly, with the two leading men being apart at the end. Why would I want to watch that? I had lived it.

I went back to Elvis and settled on *Girls! Girls! Girls!*, which I had seen fourteen times before. I liked it a great deal. He was so cool.

"He is the swingingest Elvis," I told Lucy as the movie started. Legs stretched out under the thick duvet, I began to drift off, the movie I was so familiar with not holding my attention as it usually did. My mind refused to stay focused. It wanted to go in bad directions, leading me down paths of green that matched Erik's eyes, or to summer skies with a golden sun the same color as his curls.

Soon, I gave up trying to make myself watch Elvis playing a poor Hawaiian fisherman and gave into the soft lure of the hot memories. My eyes closed slowly and he was there, as always when I needed to find release. I touched my stomach gently, letting the fantasy grab me wholly. The muscles under my hand twitched. My cock stirred. Eager and attentive, it began to fatten the longer I lay there letting erotic memory take over. Erik was on his knees inside a stall at the Moon Boy club in Helsinki. Back to the door, I lifted his curls from his brow as he sucked me off.

My hand slipped into my briefs, fisting my hard cock. I began stroking myself, each hard tug in perfect syncopation with Erik swallowing my dick. Ah, he looked so good down there. An angel come from above with his cherubic yellow hair and stunning green eyes. He took all of me down his throat. His oral skills were amazing. I pumped harder, faster, gritting my teeth as an orgasm began to build in my balls.

I told him to finish me off. He hollowed his cheeks, his gaze never leaving mine. I fucked his mouth then, long thrusts that buried my cock deeply in his throat. His sweet nose firmly resting in the thatch of dark curls at the base of my cock, he grunted and begged me visually to come, then popped off my dick with a loud slurp.

"*Da, pozhaluysta, bol'she moya lyubov'!*" I shouted. "Yes, please, more my love." My dream lover went down on me again. Held me there in his mouth and throat, eyes closed, and then pulled off slowly and held my cock as I came on his cheeks and jaw.

I thrashed around the bed like a madman, the release hard and incredibly powerful. Lucy hissed and jumped down as I clawed at the bedding with my left hand, my right tight around my cock. Hot spunk coated my fingers, palm, and the sheets. When it was over, I lay there, wet and alone, staring at the ceiling.

"*Ty, che blyad?*" I panted. "What the fuck?" I repeated in English so that Lucy could understand that I was as confused about that as she was, maybe more so. My cat only understood English, since she was an American cat. She didn't know Russian, which was why she ignored me many times when I spoke to her. Lucy leaped back onto the bed, walked over and sat on my still heaving chest.

My cat swatted my nose with a soft paw.

"Yes, you are wise. Hit me harder."

Maybe it would knock Erik out of my head and heart for good.

FIVE

Erik

When I woke up the next morning, I allowed myself exactly ten minutes of thinking about that freaky goal off my skate, and the fact that I'd been forced to shake hands with Stan, and that Stan had yanked his hand away so fast that I'd known exactly how he felt.

Not just from a goalie's point of view, either. I mean, it's okay for me to be scrappy around the net, blocking bounces, helping the goalie. But... I buried my face in my pillow and groaned loudly.

"Mr. Gunnarsson?" Amy's voice was loud enough to penetrate the door, and she didn't sound right. "I need help. Mr. Gunnarsson?"

I was up off the bed quicker than you could say five on four, and yanked the door open.

"What's wrong?" I demanded, looking for my son, but he wasn't in her arms and she looked as if she'd been crying. My world stopped in that moment, every terrible scenario I'd ever considered since becoming a dad ripping through me like wildfire. I shook her, shouted at her, pushed past her, and sprinted for Noah's room, sliding to an unglamorous halt right next to his crib.

He was there, my beautiful baby boy, sleeping, one chubby hand up by his face, the other in a loose fist on top of the blanket. He was breathing, I could see his little chest rising, and god, the nights I'd sat next to him watching for that simple sign he was okay. I'd never known that having a baby would turn my heart inside out and make me carry so much fear with me every day.

"Mr. Gunnarsson," Amy said from the door, and I turned to face her, angry that she'd scared me, even though I knew that was irrational. I took in a few things at once. She looked like shit, bless her, her long dark hair scraped back in a ponytail, her skin pale, and she was carrying a bowl that I recognized from the kitchen. "I think I'm going to…"

She didn't finish, only groaned and vomited into the bowl, then left the doorway. I was torn. Amy was clearly ill, and she was not much more than a kid herself, fresh out of college, looking for work. Should I go after her, be some kind of father figure despite being only a few years older than her, hold her hair, that kind of thing? So, with Noah sleeping, I did just that. I followed her, helped her, did all the gross things I'd gotten used to with Noah. I mean, sick, a full diaper, milk, I could do it all now.

"Should I call a doctor?"

"No, I don't think I should have eaten the—" She was sick again and never did finish the sentence. Whatever it was she had eaten, I selfishly hoped I hadn't had any of it, because missing practice today after last night's debacle was not on my to-do list.

So I helped her as much as I could, and found out it had been reheated rice, and no I hadn't eaten that, because

I'd been sulking in my room with a sleeping baby on my chest watching replays of the game.

"I'm sorry, Mr. Gunnarsson," she said pathetically as I helped her to her room. It didn't matter how many times I told her to call me Erik, she always reverted to using my last name. She said it was respectful; I just thought it was way harder to say a last name like mine than a simple Erik. I left her water, a clean bowl, and her cell phone, with orders to call the doctor if she needed to.

Shutting her door, I leaned back against it and surveyed the tiny place I'd rented. Yes, it had three rooms, but it was in the middle of nowhere. Yes, it had a kitchen, but the carpets needed replacing. Noah was already crawling and cruising the furniture, and I'd wanted more for him. Closing my eyes, I joined everything together, even though I didn't mean to—the loss last night, my goal, being unable to provide the home that Noah deserved, and the weight of blackness was heavy on me.

Then I heard it, Noah burbling away, and the world righted itself in an instant. He was my everything. Equally, it hit me straight between the eyes: I had practice in two hours. I had a baby. And no nanny.

Fuck. My. Life.

With expert-level on packing for a trip out with Noah achieved, we were on the road. I'd changed twice already today, once because Amy had got a little sick on me, and the second because Noah had found a new game of fling-ing-the-cereal-and-milk-right-at-Daddy. The world was conspiring to make my morning from hell worse, but at the stoplight I reached over to Noah in his reverse baby seat, and he gripped my thumb tight, blinking at me with those huge green eyes.

"You and me, buddy," I said.

"Bah," he said back.

"Yeah, yeah, bah."

We made it to Capital Ice Complex with half an hour to spare. I'd got there, yep, and my gear was inside the arena. But I had a baby with me. My mom's words were right front and center. *How fucking stupid are you? You think it's easy having a baby? What the hell were you thinking? Get your money back, you stupid boy.* Of course, the words had been in Swedish, and I was loosely translating "stupid boy". She'd never understood why I wanted Noah, why I'd given every cent I had to get him, and she'd officially resigned from being my mom, in a way that I wasn't sure we'd ever get back from. Dad wasn't interested; he had a new family to worry about. One of the perks of being a famous Swedish hockey player was the abundance of women willing to take Mom's place when she finally kicked him out for his whoring NHL ways.

"You and me, bud," I began, and traced a finger down his cheek, "we are not dysfunctional. Me and you? We are the dictionary definition of a functional family unit."

Having done all the woe-is-me shit, I pulled my shoulders back and lifted Noah out of the car. Fuck knew what I was going to be facing in there—a locker room full of noise, a coach who would stare at me with an expression of horror. No one brought their kids to the ice for practice. That was reserved for family skate days, and I'd missed that, as it had happened the week before I got there.

I passed through security and faced my first hurdle.

"Is that a baby?" Pete asked, and reached out to pat Noah's head. I held Noah close. Pete is one of those big security guys, all muscle, and he had a left sleeve tattoo which he flashed when he wasn't bundled up against the cold. "Intimidating" would be a good word to describe Pete, and no one tried to get past him without his say-so.

"Pete, meet Noah, my son," I said proudly.

"Aww, he's cute," Pete said, and I probably beamed at him; I did that a lot when people told me Noah was cute. Clearly Noah was the cutest, most fabulous baby in the entire world, but then I was biased. "He must look like his momma huh?" Pete asked, and left the question hanging. No way was I opening that can of worms; it was bad enough I'd brought Noah to work with me.

The main doors opened, a gust of cold air preceding two players talking loudly about something to do with potatoes. Pete was distracted, and I escaped his all-seeing gaze. I got exactly one corridor through before I met the next hurdle.

"Is that a baby?" Arvy asked. "Is that *your* baby?"

"Noah." Proudly, I lifted the soft blanket so Arvy could see more of Noah's face. I could see the moment when he saw the big eyes and the soft skin, and Arvy just sighed and cooed, and that was pretty much it.

Then he ruined the moment. "Where's your nanny?" he asked, and looked past me, expecting to see a nanny waiting there.

"Sick," I said, because I needed to be honest with Arvy so I could get help. He knew my parents were in Sweden, didn't know the full extent of my disenchantment with them both, but he realized my support network here in the US was at zero.

"Shit," he said, which, let's face it, wasn't that helpful.

Ten arrived at the little group. "Hey," he said, "is that a baby?"

"Noah," I explained as Ten cooed over Noah. Arvy looked at me pointedly, then nodded in the direction of the locker rooms and the ice.

"I didn't know what to do," I said.

"You have no backup?" Arvy asked.

Dieter and Adler walked up. "Is that a baby?" they

asked in unison. I wondered if maybe I should invest in a sign that announced that yes, Noah was a baby.

"Yes, it's a baby," I explained.

"Was he left outside in a box or something?" Adler asked with his usual lack of filter.

"Dude." Ten thumped Adler. "This is Gunner's baby, Noah."

Adler peered at Noah, and Noah batted at him with a tiny fist, wrinkling his nose. To be fair, if Adler was up in my space I'd be wrinkling my nose and making a fist as well.

When Jens and Charlie joined the group, oohing and aaahing then starting on bawdy jokes about my sex life, I was kind of done.

"I'll go talk to management," Arvy said, with a firm hand on my shoulder. "Get you some help."

He left, and the rest were still crowded around me. Five guys all joking and laughing, and Noah was restless in my arms. Hockey players weren't exactly known for their sensitivity and ability to whisper, and I wasn't sure Noah was happy.

And then it happened. Stan arrived in a swirl of cold and hostility when he looked at me. He couldn't get by the small knot of people, and I couldn't turn away, and his face was thunderous and twisted in a scornful glare. Then it changed. As if someone had waved a magic wand and wished it so, the scowl dropped, and in its place was a soft smile.

"You bring Baby-Erik," he said, then he must have realized Noah's predicament, the way he was screwing up his face ready to cry and the guys all crowding around. "Enough," he said, loudly enough to stop my team mates talking. "Space for baby. Go away."

Everyone scattered; no one wanted to argue with the

Russian who loomed large over the group. Which just left him and me in the corridor. And Noah, of course.

"This is Noah," I explained.

"His pretty," Stan said, then frowned again. "Is boy, not pretty, like handsome."

He held out his hand to Noah, who gripped a thumb tight and pulled it toward his mouth.

"*Nyet*," he murmured, "big dirty hockey man."

Noah burbled something along the lines of *bah bah*, and Stan's smile widened.

"I hold?" he asked.

I hesitated a bit. This was Stan. He hated me, and he wanted my baby to hold, and he'd just come off the street and was cold, and hell, this was my baby.

He must have seen my hesitation, because the smile slipped and he nodded. "Is okay," he said, and made to move away.

Which was when the balance tipped and I kind of thrust Noah at him, using my own baby to stop him walking off.

Stan stopped and took Noah, at first holding him under his arms, little legs dangling and kicking.

"Bah," Noah explained.

"*Mal'chik-zaichik*," Stan murmured, and instead of holding him at arm's length, he cradled him close. Right up to the thick jacket with the furry hood, and god, even at nine months, Noah looked so tiny in Stan's big, capable hands. "*Mal'chik-zaichik*," he repeated.

I leaned in. I couldn't help it; Stan's Russian had always made me weak at the knees. When we'd been together, when he'd been deep inside me as we made love, he'd talked to me and I'd melted. He could have been reciting a grocery list and it wouldn't have mattered. His soft tones and the beautiful words had never failed to push me over the edge.

"What are you saying to him?" I asked.

"Little rabbit," he said, and touched the furry ears of Noah's tiny sweater. "*Mal'chik-zaichik.*"

Oh god. I was turned on. Seriously, the voice, the beautiful hands, the way he was holding Noah, and my heart was dancing in my chest.

"He likes you," I said as Noah reached for any part of Stan he could find.

"Bah," Noah pointed out, and laughed when Stan chuckled, the sound from deep in his chest.

"Is clever," Stan said, and leaned down to press a kiss to Noah's head. "Noah."

He handed Noah back just as Arvy arrived back with someone in a suit and our captain, Connor Hurleigh, in tow.

"Eddie said he'd take him," Arvy explained. I looked from Stan to Connor and then to Arvy.

"Who is Eddie?" I asked. I wasn't going to be handing my baby over to some stranger.

The guy in the suit held out a hand.

"I'm Eddie," he said as I shook it awkwardly with Noah in my arms. "I'm here teaching Larson and Anatoly's kids. I'm police-checked, healthy, and the eldest of five, so I'm good with babies."

"He is good," Arvy said, and I stared at my fellow Swede, trying to keep the panic from my eyes. I don't know what I'd thought I would do. Skate around with Noah strapped to my back or something?

"We're not exactly set up for babies, but we could make up a corner of the room with blankets and things…"

Eddie was talking. Stan was staring at me. Arvy was

smiling, and Connor was looking at his watch and frowning.

Practice. I had to trust that the team knew this Eddie guy. "Can you get the stuff from the car for Noah?" I asked Arvy and handed over the keys.

"Is good thing for little rabbit," Stan said, and left.

I watched him walk away, wanted to call him back. Irrationally, I felt like I needed him to check out this little space for Noah with me, because I needed someone.

Anyone.

I COULDN'T HELP WORRYING, even when halfway through practice Eddie came and sat behind the glass with Noah in his arms. Noah was asleep, and Eddie gave the thumbs up. I'd already taken a puck to the shin for not concentrating, which was pissing off Coach and which would get me benched if I didn't watch out.

"Heads up, for god's sake, Gunner, keep your fucking eyes on the puck."

I attempted to ignore Eddie and Noah, and waited my turn for the shots on goal. One day I would actually get a goal past Stan, because I'd never managed it yet in any kind of practice. Even when we'd messed about at the conditioning place with street hockey, he'd never once let his net get any sign of one of my shots. Eddie had lifted Noah up against the glass, Noah's hand flat on it. My turn came up. I skated the length of the ice, deked, feinted, did everything I fucking could.

Stan stopped it. As I'd known he would.

On my way back to the group, I stopped and pressed my own gloved hand against Noah's, and he wrinkled his nose at me and bounced in Eddie's arms.

The whole team copied me; seemed like touching the glass by Noah had become a thing. Stan stopped my second shot, my third. Only Connor and Ten managed to get by him, and I wasn't in their league for accuracy.

One day.

"What's the story with Eddie?" I asked Arvy when he put Noah back in the seat and vanished from the rink side.

"Larson said he moved around so much that he and his wife wanted a private tutor for their kids, then Anatoly said maybe we should have a study room, so the kids would get stability and friends in the same position. Eddie's been here a year now—good guy."

When I collected Noah at the end of practice, I didn't expect nearly every member of the team to say goodbye, but somehow I did expect Connor to corner me. Being the captain and all that.

"You need some help finding care?" he asked. "We can find someone for you if you need that."

"My nanny is sick."

"And if she's sick again?"

"I'll deal with it, find backup." I wanted to say that it was none of Connor's business, but it was—he was captain, and he was only looking out for the team, and for me.

"He's a good baby," Connor said, petting Noah's head gently. "And how do you feel about the game last night?"

"Shit," I said, then cast a look down at Noah, ready to apologize. Noah was asleep, his lips parted, and I loved him so much.

"Don't take it to heart. You're a valuable part of this team. Work with your line and Stan, clean up those passes, keep it crisp and clean."

I nodded, then Connor left with one more tiny touch to Noah.

I'd made it almost all the way to the car, Noah bundled up in his coat, when Stan silently fell in next to me. He didn't want to talk to me, though. This was all about Noah.

"Bye, *Mal'chik-zaichik*," he murmured.

And then he walked off.

"Seriously?" I called after him. He stopped and turned. "Where's my goodbye?"

Stan pressed a hand to his chest and looked at me like the world had fallen away under his feet.

"In here, your goodbye," he said, and left without looking back.

SIX

Stan

Holding little Noah had made me feel something like nostalgia, or maybe a yearning to go back to when life was easier. Sitting at home, with Lucy on my lap, I realized that I felt homesick for the first time in many years. I missed my mother and sister. My family. Yes, the Railers were like my brothers in a way—some days fun and some days annoying—but they were not family. They didn't cook for me or smile when I walked in the door after a bad game.

I wanted that here in America. I wanted my mother here, far away from the decaying old town she clung to. Maybe when Galina arrived we could talk and plan. Come up with a way to lure my mother off the farm and into a 747. I wanted Galina nearby. I wanted a husband and children. Maybe a dog. I would have to discuss the dog idea with my cat first, though.

Lucy purred steadily, kneading the denim covering my thighs. My in-home music system was playing Russian folk music, not Elvis, for today I needed to feel connected to something, and that was my homeland, and the people dear to me that it held. The music was deeply rooted in the Orthodox Church, which I had been raised in. I'd not attended services for many years even though there was a Russian Orthodox church here in the city.

My church did not accept men such as me. I missed the services greatly, but would have felt out of place knowing the priests in their flowing black robes thought I was a perverse distortion and that I should never marry or raise children.

Pah. I felt miserable. So I dug my phone out of my back pocket and called my mother.

She greeted me with tears of joy, so happy to hear my voice. Truly it hadn't been that long since we had spoken, maybe a week, but mothers cry easily.

We talked about my sister and her arrival here in several hours. Then I begged her to come over yet again. Said I would buy the tickets and meet her at the airport, just as I'd done for my sister.

"But Stanislav, I do not like planes. If God had meant for us to fly…"

"He would have given us wings," I finished for her, both of us speaking in rapid Russian.

"Yes, see, you know that to be the truth."

"Mama, America is amazing! I have a big house. You could have your own room with air conditioning, a big TV with a thousand channels, and a Jacuzzi bath just for you. You'd not have to cook or clean, just sit back and be a queen!"

"I'll not be a bother."

"You're not a bother. Galina and I worrying about you all alone in Leskovo is a bother."

"I'm sorry for making life more difficult for you."

And now I felt guilty. "Mama, you're not. I just… I want you here. I miss my family. If you don't want to live with me, I'll get you an apartment. Harrisburg is a wonderful city! You could live by yourself. I would pay your bills and rent. Please, Mama, think about it, for me."

"I will think on it."

I knew she wouldn't. I wasn't sure what it would take to tempt her from the homeland, but it would be more than her son pleading and begging. We talked for a long time, touching on the few old friends who, like my mother, refused to leave Leskovo and live somewhere else. Then we talked about the pain in her hip. I told her that was probably because she had arthritis starting and that the old house was not warm enough for her joints.

"You should go now. Get ready for your hockey game," Mama replied.

I sighed theatrically. "And you should pack your bags and come to America so I can take care of you. You worked so hard all those years for me to play hockey. Let me repay you."

"Parents suffer; that is our lot. Now go and play good hockey for me. When you call next, I want to talk to you and Galina at the same time."

"Yes, Mama, we can do that."

"Goodbye, my sweet boy."

"Goodbye, Mama."

I tossed my phone aside and listened to Russian music until it was time to return to the arena for another game. I rode the bus in and was fine. Why my friends thought riding the bus was so bad, I didn't understand. People were nice to me. They asked me for my autograph and we talked hockey during the ride. I liked moving among the fans and people of this good city. They'd accepted me openly even when I still spoke chopped-up English.

THE DRESSING ROOM was loud when I entered after our win against Tampa Bay. Life was good. We had played well, and I had blocked forty-two out of forty-two shots. I was number one star of the game. Also, I was an hour away from seeing my baby sister. My fellow Russian strode up to me as I removed my sweaty jersey.

"Stanislav, we are thinking you should invite Erik to your party," Anatoly declared so loudly that Erik had to hear. The people in the parking lot probably heard. "To show world there is no hard feelings and team is happy good like brothers."

I threw a look at Erik. He had his back to us. His white dress shirt clung to his damp back. Those curls were just beginning to dry. In a few moments, they would bounce up into golden rings of soft satin that I could—

"*Nyet.*"

"Stan, come on, dude. Don't be mad at him. Flukes happen, right?" Tennant said while pulling on a dark brown jacket. "Could have been me or Arvy or Adzee. Just a wrong-place-wrong-time situation."

"Ten's right, Stan." I ignored Adler the best I could. "He's already feeling left out. Just invite him."

"I have numbers of foods catering counted." That was a lie and it tasted bad.

Anatoly gave me a look. A dark one. "Stanislav, New Year's is most important. Forgive bad mistake goal from Gunner. Be big man. Captain says team is family. You leave brother out of party plans?"

"I *am* big man. Go make poops in other pond."

They all stared at me. "Dude, that's a total butchery of something that was *maybe* English," Tennant finally said.

"If you wish him, fine, go tell him he has good wills. But only because it is New Year's and he has baby Noah."

I spun from them, ripped my Under Armour off, and

flung it into my stall. One of the equipment managers picked up after us, so he'd find it and wash it for me so it would be there clean and dry for the next game. I usually liked to place everything in order but today that wasn't happening.

"You be big man," Anatoly said as Tennant jogged over to pass along my invitation. Erik listened, nodded, then gave me a quick look. I returned to dressing.

"Okay, so why is New Year's such a big deal to Russians?" Adler asked, because Adler asks whatever is on his mind. I waved at Anatoly to explain before I butchered something else that might have been good English. Also, I had to catch a taxi and get to the airport to pick up my sister.

"Back when Bolsheviks come to power, religious holidays are outlawed. Christmas was banned, so people simply shift from Christmas to New Year's. Was not easy transition. Fir trees and Father Frost now could have no religious meaning. But our people are strong and smart. We make New Year's Day a day of presents and celebrations."

"What kind of jerkwad outlaws Christmas? Ouch! Shit, Ten." Adler yelped. I chuckled at the swat to the head my friend gave my other friend. "What was that for?"

"Go find Layton and have him explain. By the way, Erik said he's not sure he can make it because of needing a babysitter but he'll try."

"Whatever good," I said as I stepped into my dress slacks.

"Tennant, are you ready?" We all looked at the door at the sound of Coach Madsen's voice. My friend Tennant smiled at us, then left with his boyfriend.

Erik left then as well, and I continued dressing as Anatoly and I chatted about the party. He would oversee the bar and I was the food man. Much vodka had been purchased, he informed me.

"Oh, I see Dieter in showers. He says he brings pretty figure skating boyfriend up from Philadelphia for party tomorrow night."

"Trent is nice man." I tugged my jacket on, grabbed my bag, said goodbye to my countryman, and ran to the doors. Peter said hello, and I replied this time, stopping just for a minute to make chitter-chat before jogging out into the cold for my waiting cab. The ride to the airport seemed to take an eternity.

My sister stood just inside the doors of the Harrisburg International Airport. I ran from the parked taxi, and she met me outside. I swept her up off the ground, hugging her tightly. She was crying and gasping, her long dark hair blowing around in a bitter-cold wind.

"*Sladkaya detskaya sestra.*" "My sweet baby sister" I whispered, kissing her damp cheeks. Galina finally broke free from my embrace, laughing and crying. She grabbed my hand as the taxi driver put her bags into the trunk of the cab.

We climbed into the back of the car, glad for the warmth, and simply stared at each other for several moments. She was so beautiful, with smoky gray eyes like mine and dark brown hair. Her smile was brilliant and white, her skin soft and smooth like rich cream, and her lips as pink as the marble floors in the Kremlin throne room. She was tall, but not as tall as me, and filled out nicely now. For many years, she was thin. Too thin. Her purging disorder had made her sick, but I had paid for her recovery from my KHL monies. Now she was healthy again.

Galina was funny and loud on occasion, drank almost

as well as I could, loved rock music and dancing. She was my darling baby sister, and I adored her.

It had been some time years since we had seen each other. When I had been signed by the Railers from the KHL, I'd had to leave her behind. There was no way then for her to come because she was entering her first year as a student at Novosibirsk Medical University, studying psychology to become an eating disorder counselor. That had been her dream after recovering from her dark times. Mine was hockey in America. Hockey paid for her dream to come true. Now she was in her third year of study and always at the top of her class. My gift to her this year was plane tickets to America for a long visit.

"Tell me how you are doing."

I began to tell her.

"Tell me in English," she said, her English so much better than mine. She had taken classes in college.

"I am doing groovy good."

She laughed warmly. "Who is teaching you English? Is it an old coach?"

"No, it is Elvis movies, TV Land, and team."

"Elvis movies?" She laughed hard then. I didn't mind her joking with me. Hearing her laughter and seeing her lovely face made me feel as light as a cloud. We talked all the way back to Hershey. She filled me in on her life. School was hard, but she was doing well. She had no boyfriend, because every man her age that she met was a *bolvan*, or a jackass. Mama was well too, although she didn't see her as much as she would like. We both worried over our mother out there in that old, dead village.

"Someday I wish to bring her to America," I told her as we pulled into my driveway.

Galina gaped at my house through the steamy windows. "Stanislav, your house is huge!"

"But empty until you come to visit."

We ran inside, me pulling her along, anxious to show her my new American house. Then I ran back out to pay the cab driver and gather her many bags. I gave her a tour and got her settled into a guest room. We changed into pajamas and then watched Elvis movies while we sipped icy-cold vodka and ate pickles. Lucy took turns sleeping on me and my sister. All night we spoke in English mixed with Russian, and it was joyous to let my native tongue flow freely on occasion.

"What time is it?" Galina asked after yawning widely. My head was peaceful on a pillow on the floor and I hated to lift it up, but for her, I would. "Tell me in English. You won't get better in the language if you do not use it."

"Ten after two," I replied, then rolled to my side to look up at her. She was on her belly on the big, fat sofa. Her hair was flipped up over her head and hung over her face.

"We have much work tomorrow for your party." That wasn't a question but a fact. I nodded and giggled at the silly feeling in my toes. "I am going to bed now." She began snoring.

"*Dobroy nochi*," I said, and closed my eyes. Galina never said goodnight in return before I fell asleep on the floor. I had to get up the next morning. The skate was optional, but I was hoping Galina would take over talking to caterers and decorators and who knows what.

When I woke up, I walked into the chaos of getting ready for the party.

I scooped up Lucy, who was cowering behind the sofa, and put her in a cat box ready to take her to the vets for her overnight stay. I needed to get out of here and together we would find peace, and hope that when we came back all would be well.

SEVEN

Erik

"Hey, we haven't met."

I looked up from lacing my skates, and the cutest, sweetest, shortest woman stood there, with her hands on her hips and a toddler by her side. I remembered my manners and clambered to stand, but she held up a hand to stop me.

"Don't get up," she said, and even her voice was little in the locker room.

"No, ma'am." She might be tiny, but she had a way about her that I didn't want to argue with. "Hi," I said to the little girl standing confidently next to her mom.

"Hi, I'm Ellie, and my dad is in charge of you," she announced imperiously. Was this the daughter of someone in management? I looked to her mom for clarification, and she smiled at me and held out a hand.

"Liza Hurleigh. I'm Connor's wife."

Oh. *That kind of boss*; the captain of the Railers.

"Ma'am," I said again, and shook her hand, which was so small in mine.

"Connor said you have a baby and that you might need

some help right now?" She tilted her head, and Ellie did as well, like a mini-me. "We have a group of WAGs and a kind of co-operative on emergency childcare. Connor says you have a nanny?"

"Yes ma'am."

"Liza, please. If you give her this information, she can connect with some of the moms and nannies, and then if the worst happens you know someone always has your back." She handed me a card, and I took it without even looking at it.

I blinked up at her, not entirely sure what to say. It seemed too good to be true, but didn't I need a wife or girl-friend to qualify? Certainly, I didn't have a WAG, nor would I ever, but explaining that right now? I couldn't do that, even if the Railers whole team appeared to be coming out. Well, not the whole team, but at least two, anyway.

"That sounds wonderful, ma— Liza."

"Good, good," she said, as if that was one more thing she had to cross off her list of good deeds today. "Tell her she can call anytime, or you can, and we can set up a play date."

"Noah isn't one yet," I said, but that didn't seem to be an obstacle for one of these play dates.

"A baby." She smiled so widely. "And it's never too soon to have play dates. I guess I'll see you tonight, at Stan's party?"

"I'll be there," I lied; I hadn't made up my mind yet. Amy was over her sickness thing, and she'd said she had Netflix she needed to catch up on and added that I paid her for her skills at sitting with a baby and watching TV on New Year's. Thing was, balancing the concept of facing Stan with the idea of snuggle-time with Noah... I knew which was winning.

Liza left with a goodbye, and Ellie trailed after her. It was only as they left that I realized I hadn't known that play dates for little babies were even a thing. I mean, what did they do? Throw cereal at each other? Crawl and bump into furniture?

Let's face it, I am a shit dad.

With that stuck in my craw, I laced my skates fully and grumbled my way out onto the ice. Only Connor and my line mates Toly and Charlie were on the ice, and I blurted out the first thing I thought of when Connor skated over to me.

"Dude, your wife is tiny; you must be able to…" I stopped, and he raised an eyebrow, clearly asking for the rest of the sentence. "…pick her up," I ended.

"Did she tell you about the WAGs and the cooperative care backup?"

"She did."

"Good." He skated away slowly, and the three of us, the Erik/Toly/Charlie line, stopped in front of him. "All we're working on today is some passing skills. I notice that Erik is faster and…"

The rest of the session, or at least half of it, passed in slow motion checking of positions for passes, and I enjoyed it to the point where I could have done it all day.

Skate. Netflix and snuggle with Noah. Bed. No party at all. Perfect day.

"Okay, guys, I think we're done."

"Is not done." A booming voice came from behind us, and I couldn't help myself; I had to turn around to see if maybe it was another Russian on the ice with us. No, luck wasn't on my side. Stan, in full gear, was heading for his net, and when he passed there was a constant stream of Russian.

"Thought you were organizing party," Toly said, and leaned on his stick.

Stan came to a halt, snowing the net, then turned to face us, skating to the left and stopping, and then to the right, scoring up the ice in the blue paint. He said something to Toly in Russian, and Toly answered back with a huff of laughter.

"Big chaws," Stan announced, and hit the post gently with his stick, like a love tap. "Sister is all yell, and pussy mad. I leave. Shoot puck." He took a stance, and it wasn't just me staring at Stan and not quite getting what he'd said.

"Did he say chaws?" Charlie asked.

"What is chaws?" Connor asked us, and then he raised his voice. "What is chaws, Stan?"

Stan scowled. "Mess, noise."

Connor looked at us blankly, and then I could see a dawning realization on his face. "Chaos," he said. "I think he means chaos."

"Chaws," Stan repeated. "Is what I say. Shoot."

"I'm out of here," Connor announced, "See you all tonight."

He fist-bumped us, and I looked at the other two expectantly. If they went as well, then I could go without feeling like a complete shit.

"I'm in if you are," Charlie said.

"Me also," Toly added.

"Yeah," I said, "me too."

One by one, we attempted single shots on goal, gently at first, letting Stan warm up, until the Russian he was shouting was less words than these weird humming noises he sometimes made when he was in that place. Yep. Stan was in the zone.

We practiced a rush, passing between us, and Charlie

managed to get a goal past Stan. "Is good," he shouted, and poked at Charlie with his stick. "You make good Russian."

Charlie puffed up at that, and chirped at me as he went past. "I'm good," he said in a bad attempt at a Russian accent. "You're shit." He ducked my head-rub and we went for another rush. This time I was shooting, but Stan was there, catching it as though I'd just tossed it to him and not blistered a slap shot right at him.

"Is bad," he jeered, and Charlie repeated that as I went back. I knew Charlie was teasing, but the doubts inside me were like an acid eating away at my control. The next rush, I was an assist on a goal made against Stan, this time by Toly, who went down on his knees and slid a third of the way across the ice in mock celebration.

"Get the fuck up," I snapped, and he did, but not without showering us with ice from his jersey. Bastard.

"Toly is good Russian," Stan summarized.

We rushed again. I was determined to get a shot past him, and we were at speed, aiming right for the big guy in net. I could see the goal, visualize the puck in the net. I wound up, looked Stan right in the eyes, tilted so it looked like I was going five hole, and then slam, right in the net over his head. I began to celebrate, then realized that Stan was holding the puck.

"Too easy," he chirped at me.

"Again," I snapped to my line mates, and even though they exchanged looks that spoke volumes about me being out of my freaking mind, they went for it. We skated so fast at Stan that I couldn't stop myself from barreling into him. A normal man would have been flat on the floor. A normal goalie wouldn't have been knocked to the ground and still have the damn puck in his glove.

I pushed at the weight of him pinning my leg, and he rolled off, and it sounded like he was laughing.

"You easy like broken car."

God knew what that meant. I didn't care. All the tension of moving here, sitting in a crappy apartment, hiring a nanny I could ill afford, worrying about Noah, paying off my ex, and I was done.

So done.

"Again."

Two more times Stan stopped me. He was reading me better than I could read myself.

"Try hard bad," Stan informed me when I pushed off the board behind the net. What was wrong with me? Why was I not getting this? I'd beaten goalies, so many of them. I was a good skater, I worked hard, I was accurate.

I iced to a stop next to Toly and Charlie. Toly pointed up at the clock, but didn't say anything. We needed to get off the ice.

"One more," I said.

They didn't argue, must have seen something in me that spoke of utter focus, and we set off again. This time, though, it wasn't Stan in the net, it was just some random goalie, and when I took the pass, crisp and clean from Toly, I visualized the net—not the puck going in, but the space —and when the puck left my stick, I knew it would get past him. My momentum carried me on to him, and I skated hard left to avoid being part of a Stan/net sandwich. I didn't have to see the puck go in. I just knew.

Charlie tapped the ice with his stick in celebration, and grinned widely. "Now can we go? Toly only has a few hours to try to look pretty."

"Fuck you," Toly said without heat, and the two of them skated off. I waited for Stan, flushed with success and a hint of pride.

"I let in," Stan said as he skated past, but I was on him and in front of him in an instant, blocking his exit off the ice.

"You did not let that in. It was a solid goal."

Stan shrugged. "I let in," he repeated.

Everything stood between us, like a brick wall; the fact that I'd walked away, that I had never contacted him, that I'd chosen a wife instead of him. It was all there, and I hated every pound of the weight between us.

"I'm sorry, okay?" I shouted at him.

He just looked at me, confused, then nodded. "Don't tug tail of tiger."

"What?"

"Tiger, tail." Stan frowned and muttered something in Russian. "Angry," he summarized, like that made it all better.

That made no fucking sense and, frustrated, I couldn't help everything spilling out. I pressed a gloved hand to his chest and pushed so he'd feel me. "What can I do? To make things right?"

"Time," Stan murmured after a few moments' consideration. "Big time."

I skated aside to let him through, and he walked off to the locker rooms. For half an hour I skated slow circles and figures of eight, waiting until I knew the locker room would be empty, and fucking glad there were no kids' lessons on New Year's. It meant I had the place to myself, and I could think.

When I looked at Stan, I saw the man I'd fallen in love with, his strength and passion and utter determination, and I missed him.

Grief spiked me so hard I slid to a stop by the boards.

"Everything okay?" a voice asked.

I looked up to see Pete the security guy looking at me as if I was an alien.

I huffed a laugh. Was I okay? Not today, no, but maybe Stan was right. With time, maybe I'd be fine and guilt wouldn't be my constant friend.

"I'm good," I lied.

"I think they want to close the place," Pete said.

"Yeah, sorry, I'll be out in thirty."

"No sweat."

When I got to the locker room, there was no sign of Stan, Toly or Charlie. I showered quickly, dressed in my street clothes and hurried out to my car.

I needed some Noah time. Badly.

AMY HELD out her hands for Noah. She'd been poking at me to go to this damn party all through the hours between getting home and now. I didn't want to hand him over. He was my barrier against the rest of the world, and I was happy and content just sitting there with him.

"We'll be fine," she said.

I knew that. I trusted her. She'd been recommended to me, and I liked her. She was good for Noah and me, and the little guy needed that. But she was wrong about the party. After the ice incident, I wasn't that keen on making nice with the team.

All because I couldn't make nice with Stan.

"This is team bonding," she said. Again.

I knew that. I knew it was bonding. I mean, what was more bonding than getting blind drunk with your team mates? Only I hadn't had a drink since Freja had told me she was pregnant. First it had been the shock that one drunken hookup had produced a child, then it had been solidarity with her, then it had been because I was determined to be the most responsible dad in the entire world. Now it was because I'd lost the habit of cracking a cold one.

"Noah is sleepy, so am I, you need to go."

I looked at my wide-awake son and my equally non-sleepy nanny and sighed.

"I'll take a shower," I agreed grudgingly.

A shower became needing a shave first, and then styling my hair, and then finding clean, presentable jeans and a smart button-down shirt in a dark red. Only when I passed the mirror did I realize what I'd done. I looked good, even for me, but was it for Stan, or was it for the team?

Maybe it was just for me?

I kissed Noah, fussed with him a little, and he did at least let out a tiny yawn.

I handed Amy the card Liza had given me, said I'd explain it all tomorrow but that this was kind of a back-up for her. She just said she had my cell phone number, and added that just because she'd got food poisoning once didn't mean it was going to happen again.

"I'll call in," I said as I walked through the door.

She shut the door on me, and I kind of needed that. Because standing outside the apartment debating whether to stay or go, with the door open wide, wasn't a good thing.

My car started first time, it wasn't snowing, and I made it to Stan's place in good time. He had a typical highly paid player NHL house, all gates and walls and wide turning areas for cars. There weren't a lot of cars there, but I knew most of the guys were taking cabs, and some were actually staying the night.

For a while I sat in my car looking up at the house. Don't tug a tiger by the tail. I'd looked it up, or at least I'd looked up what I thought Stan had meant. Don't make Stan angry, because he might turn on me. That was the only meaning I could ascertain.

If only I could turn back the clock to last year. Instead of just leaving I would have explained more, about expectations on me, and about how I felt.

I would have still left, but at least my heart wouldn't feel quite so bruised.

A loud knock on the window had me jumping so hard I smacked my head on the roof of the car.

"Way to give me a concussion, asshole," I said to Arvy when I opened the door.

"Get your ass inside—it's fucking freezing out here."

So I did. I walked inside with Arvy, and there was Stan looking like he'd stepped off the pages of a fashion magazine. He was so gorgeous I nearly went to my knees at the thought of what I'd lost with the decisions I'd made.

"Vodka," he announced, and thrust a glass at each of us. *"Na Zdorovie,"* he said, jovially. "Drink."

And for the first time in a long time, I drank.

EIGHT

Stan

"What's the difference between a G-spot and a golf ball?" Adler shouted over the thumping rap music someone had turned on.

Who had done that? What was wrong with Elvis? Ugh. Rude people. I shrugged because I didn't know what a G-spot was. My sister began to snicker. Arvy continued staring at my sister. He had been doing that for the past hour since he had arrived with Erik. My gaze kept leaping from Adler to Erik, who was talking to Dieter and Trent by the food table.

"A guy will actually search for a golf ball."

Galina threw back her head and laughed heartily. I chuckled to be polite. Adler rolled his eyes.

"Didn't you get it?" Adler asked. Galina patted my biceps.

I shrugged. "I am not sure for this G-spot is," I confessed.

My sister rose to her toes and whispered into my ear what a G-spot was and where it was located. I felt my face turn hot. That made Galina laugh again.

"My brother has always been a shy one when it comes to female things," she said with a smile. Arvy stared at her openly. I peeked over my sister's head and saw Erik break away from Trent and Dieter to go upstairs.

"Tell more jokes. They are funny. Ha!" I moved around Adler while keeping my focus on Erik. He climbed the stairs quickly. Was he getting his coat from the blue guest room and leaving? Why? I had not glowered at him at all. Moving past the large fir tree, I grabbed the present I had run out to buy for his baby and went off after him. Tennant and Jared slowed me down by the buffet table asking about the pickled herring, why there was so much salami, and what the beet-and-potato salad dressed with olive oil was. I hurried to answer them as nicely as I could, then ran up the stairs, gift in hand.

I checked all the bedrooms and didn't find him. Leaving mine, I stumbled over him in the hallway, leaving the bathroom. His green eyes flared when he saw me.

"Nice bathroom," he said, then gestured at the room.

"Yes. It has good toilet." Ugh. That was stupid. "And sink. Sink is good."

"Yeah, I saw that too. Look, Stan…"

I shoved the box with the silver paper and red bow at him. "Is for new baby."

"Noah. His name is Noah."

"Yes, I know is Noah. That is good name." I shook the present. He stood there staring at it like it might be a bear trap. "Take it."

"I'm not sure I should." He shoved his hands into the front pockets of his jeans. "I mean, it's really nice and all…"

"Take it. Our bad past no mean baby should not have gift."

He lifted a shoulder. The shirt he was wearing slid

down to show me a bit of his collarbone. It was just as beautiful as I recalled. Covered with delicate skin that would bruise if I sucked on it long and hard enough.

"He got his gifts last week."

"Then he has more." I crammed the damn box against his chest. "Why be so awful stupid? Take present for Noah. I shop hard with bad head."

His mouth tightened. "Stan, I appreciate it, but I got my son stuff for Christmas. He's good."

"He is no good before getting—this getting my...my gift for him makes happy times for baby. You are...why so always—stupid corn fucker!"

Erik snorted. My brain caught up with my words and I felt even more inept and bumbling.

"Corn fucker?" He snickered a bit. It made me incredibly upset to hear him laughing at me, like he probably had the day he'd walked away from me. Laughing at the big oaf of a Russian who had fallen so hard and so fucking deep.

"I hurt for you so much!" I shouted, grabbed a handful of those golden curls, and jerked him to me, my mouth crushing his. I kissed him hard, violently, angrily. He stiffened, then leaned in to me, just a bit. That changed the kiss from something done to hurt him into something being done for sheer pleasure. His lips softened, his mouth opened, and I went in deep. Erik moaned softly as my tongue slipped over his. The taste of him lit fires within me I'd thought long doused. My grip in his hair tightened... then Anatoly bellowed my name.

I stumbled away from him, my fingers slipping out of his hair, my lips wet from our kiss.

"Stanislav! Come break the seal on the vodka!" Toly roared to the hoots of many of the Railers in attendance.

I flung the gift at Erik and thundered down the stairs,

my face flushed. The bottle of *Beluga Noble* was handed to me, and I cracked the seal and downed several long pulls. Cheers went up. Anatoly opened a second bottle, and I drank from that one as well. I then went on to drink out of every bottle that was opened over the next hour, in the hopes that I would no longer feel the heat of Erik's kiss. It didn't work. The vodka sat in my stomach doing nothing to dull the ache in my head and heart. I tossed back shot after shot, my eyes on Erik as he was handed a shot glass. He'd hovered at the fringes of the party for the last hour, giving me sidelong glances.

He threw the vodka back like a professional, then took another shot. I sipped on my next shot, my attention on my ex-lover as he began to talk a bit more loudly and wave his arms about with more passion. I'd never seen Erik tipsy. During our summer in Helsinki, he didn't drink alcohol. Of course, during a rigorous training regime, drinking would be foolish, but on the rare nights out, he'd still drank very little. I enjoyed my vodka on occasion, such as parties and celebrations or when trying to drown the confusion Erik caused.

Another hour passed. He had taken one more shot and paired it with a beer Tennant had handed him. The guests were leaving now that two a.m. had come and gone. Galina and Anatoly had left to take Arvy home. Foolish man had tried to match my sister shot for shot and was, to quote Adler, shitfaced.

"Thank you for a wonderful time," Trent said as he bussed my cheeks. I straightened, then shook Dieter's hand. "Is anyone in charge of Curly Top over there?"

Trent pointed at Erik, stretched out on the sofa, talking to himself as he balanced a beer bottle on his nose. Or tried.

"I will take charge of him," I told the tiny man with

the big personality. Trent gave me a long look though eyes heavy with makeup. Then he winked.

"Be gentle. He looks delicate." With that, the man in the pink-and-plum suit patted my biceps, latched on to his boyfriend's arm, and led Dieter off into the bitter-cold night.

The house was in chaos. A cleaning company would come tomorrow to attend to the carnage. I stepped over paper plates and beer bottles as I made my way to the couch. Erik blinked at me around the green bottle wobbling about on his face.

"I'm a seal," he chuckled, then barked like one.

"You are drunken fool," I said, then reached down to pull him to his feet.

"I'm not drunk. I'm buzzed. Stop pulling on me. I can walk." The bottle rolled down his chest to join the others on the floor. "Is there any of that salami left?"

He shook free and staggered to where the food had been.

"All is cleaned up." I took him by the arm and led him to the stairs. "You sleep here. No drive home and kiss stop sign."

"I only kiss Russian goalies." He snorted and proceeded to trip up the first step.

I rolled my eyes and swept him off his feet, shouldering him like a sack of potatoes, and climbed the steps to the second floor.

"Oh wow, this is some view. Anyone ever tell you your ass is tight as a turtle?"

"You are drunk. Stop talking horse ass words."

He patted my backside, nickered like a horse, giggled, and made a fool of himself the entire way up the stairs and into the guest room beside Galina's. I could see why he rarely drank. He was a lightweight.

I dropped him onto the double bed, and he simply rolled out over it, no tension at being dropped from my shoulder at all.

"Where did your ass go?" He snorted as I kneeled to remove his shoes.

"Where is all time." I yanked one shoe off, then the other, and flung his rubbery legs onto the bed.

"I have to go home. To Noah."

"Noah is with nanny. No drive." I stood and leaned over him to rifle through the pockets of his pants for his keys .

He slapped a hand on the back of my neck. I glanced up from the rich blue bedding to find those jade eyes locked on me.

"I'm so sorry, Stan. For leaving you…for hurting you." His fingers bit into the nape of my neck. I was frozen in place with shock. He had no worry of me pulling away. I couldn't. "She said she would get rid of him, and there would be no Noah." His grip lightened, his fingers sliding over my neck to my ear then to my jaw. "I wish I could have both of you. I never stopped caring…never stopped wanting… never stopped…"

His eyes slipped shut. His hand dropped from my face and he began snoring lightly.

I left his room in a daze, my mind knotted. Even an hour later, as I rolled from one side to the other, after Galina had returned home and gone to bed, my thoughts were spinning. All I could think of was life and fate and chance.

Back in the old days, before the arrival of Christianity in Russia, many worshipped old gods. Among those old gods was Ustrecha, the goddess of chance. As the sun worked its way around the earth, I lay there, thinking of chance and fate. Had it been chance that had brought Erik and me together for that long, hot summer? Yes, probably. And had it been fate that had made him walk away? Did the gods of old Russia have his life laid out before them, and had they seen that he needed to be with the mother of his son to create him? And, knowing that, had they taken him from me?

Did he really still care for me? Want me? Did I dare even think about such things?

I slipped from bed when the sky was still black, grabbed my phone and Erik's keys, and snuck past the sleeping partiers. Down to the kitchen I went, chancing a peek at the clock on the wall. Five minutes after four. The kitchen was the only clean part of the house, so I settled in there, making coffee and sitting at the big island in the middle of the massive room. His keys and my phone rested by my coffee mug. I sat on a stool and drank coffee and wondered if Ustrecha was playing with me and Erik right now. Old gods enjoyed toying with people. That was well known. I drank a pot of coffee, made more, ate some toast, and returned to my seat to watch the sun pinken the winter sky, my thoughts still gnarled.

"Hey."

I glanced back over my shoulder at Erik. He looked like the bottom of a well-used toilet. His curls were matted, his eyes red, his shirt wrinkled, and his trousers twisted.

"I need my keys."

"You will eat first. Then I will give you keys."

"I need to get home to Noah."

"You need eat. No pull over police with high booze blood count. Bad for Noah if arrested."

Erik refused to argue that good point.

"I woke up and didn't know where I was," he said instead.

"Sit. You look bad like hell."

"You mean I look like hell."

I stood and he sat, dropping his forehead to the cold marble island top, then moaning. I smiled at his pain. I'd been there many times myself.

"I make food for us. Many eggs and wheat toast."

"Your English is a lot better than the last time we were…well, when we were…fuck."

I nodded and continued gathering cooking pans. "Yes, it is better. Good now. Hip and cool."

Erik smiled, then groaned. "Got any aspirin?"

"Is obvious you not Russian." I let the frying pan and eggs go for a moment. I kept aspirin in the cupboard with the glasses, so that aches and pains from hockey could be addressed as soon as I got home. Sometimes my hips ached. I dumped two white pills into my palm, got him some coffee, and walked around the island to place them both in his hand.

He lifted his head from the island, smiled, and washed down the pills with the strong black coffee.

When the pills were down, he handed me the mug. I stood there for a long time, his mug in my hand, my gaze on his beautiful face. Yes, he was still beautiful to me, even if slightly green in the gills.

"You remember what you say last night?" I had to ask. His words had clattered around inside my head like a lone pea in a pod. So many confusing things. His professions to still caring. Him saying that his girl would get rid of the baby. What did that mean? Put Noah up for adoption? Get an abortion? So many questions that needed his answers. "To me? Feeling sorry? Never stop caring? Wanting? This is true speak from you?"

"Yeah, it's true speak."

I could feel the touch of the old gods taking me in hand. I placed his mug on the island and reached for him, the back of his neck chilly against my warm fingers. Erik came willingly, eagerly perhaps, slipping off the stool as I led his mouth up to mine. Why I was doing this, I had no idea, but it felt right. As if predestined. Blessed by the fates. He lifted a bit, onto his toes. I shimmied down, my ass against the island, and his tongue came searching for mine. My fingers travelled up his neck into his hair. Those glorious curls wrapped around my hand as I suckled on his tongue, pulling a rumble out of him that I'd not heard since our time in Helsinki. The sound of pleasure set fire to me. Lust raced through my veins, quickly plumping my dick.

Erik was pliant in my arms. I pulled him close as I moved from his mouth to his long, unmarred neck. I nipped and bit, pulling some of that tender skin between my teeth. He trembled and writhed, his cock rolling over mine. I sucked in a hot breath. Erik grabbed at my sides, his fingers digging into my ribs.

"My beautiful dream man," I murmured, then moved to another spot, that luscious collarbone I had seen briefly last night. I yanked at the collar of his shirt, popping a button free. He gyrated against me, his hands now clawing at me.

"Say it in Russian," he panted.

"*Moy prekrasnyy chelovek mechty,*" I huffed, then nibbled on his collarbone. He tried pulling me closer, but there was no space left between us. I spun him around, the stool catching on his foot, or leg perhaps, and toppling over to the floor. His ass hit the island. He grunted. I continued sucking on his shoulder and neck, biting along his collarbone, reminding myself of how delicious his skin was.

He touched me first, slipping his hand into my lounge pants to find my cock. I rocked into his grip, my hands now fisted in his hair.

"Free yourself. Take us both in hand." I whispered into his ear, then tugged on the lobe with my teeth.

"Oh fuck, fuck, fuck." Erik did as he'd been told. My knees nearly folded when his cock lay next to mine in his hand. "Kiss me. Kiss me hard."

I left his ear and covered his mouth with mine, pumping in and out of his tight grip, mad with want. He gripped my hip hard with his free hand, fingertips biting painfully into my flesh. He might be smaller than me, but still he was a man, he was strong. I would carry the marks of this encounter just as he would. That thought fired me even more, and I plunged deeper into his mouth as he jerked and tugged on our cocks. My orgasm hit me quickly, as did his. He came a moment before I did, his spunk coating his hand. The slick and heat pushed me over as I imagined that his hand was his ass, tightening around me as he gasped and shuddered.

We rode out our releases, his hand gripping and pressing our cocks tight, milking us both until the trembling subsided. His brow rested on my shoulder, my nose buried in the thick mass of gold rings. I opened my eyes and saw the sun peeking through the bare trees, shining on us, reality slicing into the cloud of yearning and sex that lingered in my kitchen.

I pulled away, his fingers sliding from our slick cocks, his eyes slowly opening, showing me sated emerald beauty. I'd always gotten lost in those eyes. What did I do now? Kiss him? Shove him out the door? Take him to my bed for the rest of the day? Call him names? I was flustered, unsure, scared of the emotions trying to overtake me again.

"We have eggs now." I walked to the sink, washing my hands vigorously.

"Stan…" I heard him pulling paper towels off the holder on the island.

"We have eggs now." I cranked off the taps, grabbed the edge of the sink, and inhaled and exhaled several times. I heard his keys jingle, and craned my head to look back at him. He'd tucked and zipped and righted his shirt. He looked as good as a man who had slept in his clothes could look.

"I'm leaving now. I'll call a cab, and I just— That was… I need to get home to Noah."

"Go, then." I looked away from him and locked my gaze on the bubbles in the sink.

"I'll pick the car up another time. Stan…"

"Go. Now. Go. I am— This was bad stupid. Eggs would be stupider worse."

He left without replying. I stood there watching the bubbles disappear until the cleaning crew arrived. I wondered if they could neaten my life as well as tidying my house.

NINE

Erik

I can't help but think that somehow, at some point, I fucked up last night. After what happened between us in Helsinki, shouldn't we be able to stand and talk? I could have explained about Freja in a lot more detail, about her career, and her not wanting the baby, about the things I'd decided after she told me that.

But we'd reverted to type, falling on each other like starving animals, and there hadn't been any talking. Nothing more meaningful that harsh breathing and curse words.

And then eggs? What the hell? I should have stayed, I could have asked him why he'd turned away. Was it revulsion? Or guilt? Or just plain anger? I needed to talk to someone; that was someone who wasn't nine months old and breaking his first tooth. There was no game today, and no skate, not even an optional one, but we were back tomorrow with practice, and back-to-back road-trip games the day after that.

Road trips. No Noah, and all Stan, and this weird, impenetrable wall that was between us.

I need to talk to someone.

Freja was out. She was on location somewhere in Brazil —her first breakthrough, apparently, and the reason she hadn't reached out to visit Noah and me over Christmas. Not that I'd expected her to; as far as she was concerned, she'd had Noah, and now it was on me.

Arvy was my best bet. He knew my town, my family, the way I'd seen my own parents' marriage crumble and how I'd wanted better for Noah. He'd understand.

He was also single, and probably hungover, so he'd be at home and an easy target. I changed Noah's diaper, pulled on layers of clothes and the familiar bunny coat, and called a cab. Maybe this was the best thing. I'd talk to Arvy, get my head clear, and then get another cab, or Arvy, to drop me at Stan's so I could collect my car. If I timed it right, I might be able to talk to Stan as well.

Or eat some eggs or something.

I texted Arvy to ask for his address. He sent it back immediately, and then there was a second text. *Why?* Too late. I had the address, I had a cab booked, and Noah and I were on a road trip all of eight miles to Arvy's place.

The man who opened the door to me wasn't the one I expected. I mean, it was Arvy, but he wasn't bleary and hungover, he was bright and shiny and exuded all kinds of things like good health and cheeriness.

"Come in, come in," he said, and took Noah from me, doing a complicated back step and making Noah fly, which he loved and giggled loudly. "So, Master Noah, I have all sorts of things to tempt you with." He opened the door to his enormous fridge, which at first glance just held beer and cans of energy drinks. "Guess we need to ask Papa if he brought you any snacks, little man."

The flow of Swedish was too loud for me, but Noah,

who was used to a whole mishmash of English and Swedish, burbled and batted his hands at Arvy.

"I have this," I said, and handed over a banana. Arvy looked at it and then at Noah, puzzled, and I immediately took the banana back, opened cupboards, found a plastic bowl, and chopped the banana into finger-squishing pieces. There was no high chair here, but between us we made a nest of pillows that Arvy assured me were only cheap and could be replaced.

And then, with coffee and cookies he had at the back of a cupboard, we sat on opposite sofas.

"How do you even survive?" I asked, and indicated the fridge.

"Takeout when I don't eat at the rink. Not shitty take-out, though. There's a salad place that delivers and it's only a few miles up the road. But you're not here to quiz me on the contents of my fridge."

"I just don't have a lot of friends in Harrisburg yet, and you're the best I have, and I needed someone to listen."

"No worries, but can I go first?" Arvy sat upright and crossed his legs, his coffee perilously close to ending up on his thick cream carpets. "I think I'm in lust."

I blinked at him. "Who with?"

"I met her last night. She has beautiful dark hair, and these gorgeous gray eyes, and her smile... Beautiful."

Gah. If I hadn't known better I would have thought he was describing Stan, and then it hit me. "Stan's sister?"

"You saw her, right? Do you think I should ask her out? Would Stan kill me?"

"He loves his sister," I said. I knew that because it was what he'd told me last summer. Not told me exactly, but he'd always smiled when he mentioned her name. He was a passionately possessive Russian, Galina was his sister, and

Arvy was a hockey player, albeit a rich one. That was not going to go down well.

"I think I'll ask her, if I can, so hands off, okay? You might be single now, but I saw her first."

He was joking, but there was something in his eyes that I recognized. Connection. I'd been so lost in thinking about Stan and then drinking myself into oblivion that clearly I had missed the Arvy/Galina thing altogether. What I saw in Arvy was a serious grown-up attraction, not some puck bunny connection that wouldn't last.

"She's nice," I said, "but I need to talk to you first, if you've got time." I realized I was giving him every opportunity to back out of talking to me. All he did was settle back on the sofa and wait. Noah had nodded off, facing me, banana squished into intricate sewed patterns on one of the cushions.

"So, Noah was an accident." I wasn't sure why I started there, but the explanation had to start somewhere. "He's the product of a one-night stand when I'd drunk way too much. I'd met Freja a couple of times before, and who knows, maybe we could have dated, but we went straight to sex, and jeez…"

"Why are you telling me this?" Arvy asked, his tone serious.

"Because this was why I got married, okay? Because she came to me for money for an abortion, and I was going to give it to her, and then when it came to it I couldn't. So we came to an arrangement and she carried Noah to term, and I'm his sole parent now."

"Again, Erik, why are you telling me all this?"

Noah mumbled and blinked open his eyes, and I scooped him up, banana and all, and held him to my chest. He bobbled his head a couple of times and then he was asleep again.

"Because of Stan. Because between one night with Freja and a wedding, I had Stan."

"At the conditioning event, you mean, you met Stan? I know you did. I met Stan. Didn't understand a word he said."

"No, I was...with Stan, we had a..." What word summed up what we'd had? Relationship? Affair? "...a thing," I finished in my usual pathetic, half-hearted way of labelling what had been the most intense connection I'd had in my entire life. The same connection that had never left.

"He's, your... You mean... Jeez, what is it with this team?" He was joking to counteract the sudden seriousness of what I'd just revealed.

"I'm trusting you with this, because we grew up in the same town, and we're friends, and you know me."

Arvy nodded, then shook his head, like he couldn't make up his mind. "Clearly not as well as I thought."

"We split, me and Stan. It was supposed to be for the summer, and that was it, like a proximity thing is all, only I fell in love, and he did, and then I left him."

"Let me get this right." Arvy sat forward again, his confusion obvious. "You fell in love and you left him? Why would you..." He trailed away, and I waited for the penny to drop. Which it did quickly, because Arvy was always the clever one. "Because you found out you were going to be a daddy and decided to do what? The honorable thing? Jesus, Erik. You didn't have to get married."

"I did. Noah deserves that."

"Like he deserves divorced parents now?"

That hurt, because no child deserved an unhappy family, but too often they were in the middle of one. My childhood hadn't been the brightest in terms of parents, but I'd had hockey and friends, and now I had Noah and was determined to do things right for him.

"Do I tell everything to Stan? You've played with him all season, you know him better than I do."

Arvy raised an eyebrow, "I doubt it."

"Asshole, you know I didn't mean it that way."

"On this team, who knows?" Arvy muttered.

I ignored him. "First I think I should explain it all. Then I think, do I want him back even if he wanted me? After all, he was happy for me to walk away. What if the summer was a one-off, an affair that was always time-stamped to end when we left?"

"Jesus." Arvy stood up and stretched. "I think we need a beer."

"It's eleven a.m."

"It's five o'clock somewhere."

"Not for me, thanks."

"Sprite, then—you like that shit." He was at the fridge by then, and I got the impression the conversation was being ended on his terms.

"Arvy? What do I do?" I asked, hating that I was dumping all of this on him. He stopped with the fridge door open and his back to me. With a loud exhalation, possibly of irritation, he turned to face me.

"You visit Stan and you tell him what you told me, but in words of one syllable where possible and with the aid of diagrams. What's stopping you?"

Knowing that he could tell me to leave and that last summer meant nothing to him. Even if he did kiss me, and more, and touch my hair as if he was reaching for memories.

"I don't know," I lied.

"Do you want me to tell you not to go?"

"Maybe? No. Yes. I don't know."

Arvy placed the unopened cans on the counter and picked up his keys. "Come on, I'll take you."

"What? Now?"

"You want to wait until tomorrow when you'll have even more reasons not to talk to him, let alone the fact that we have practice and then we're getting ready for the road trip?

"No. Yes."

"Make up your mind."

I stood up, awkwardly with Noah still asleep in my arms. Stan might not even be home, and then there was the road trip, and maybe I could avoid talking to him until after then. Did I want to see how he felt now? Did I want to try to convince him that we could give everything another try? Last night he'd kissed me, got me off, and he'd wanted me so badly he was shaking with the need of it.

The sex had always been good, explosive. Enough to make me forget my own name. I looked down at a sleeping Noah.

So, I go to Stan, and I tell him everything, and what am I even looking for?

Forgiveness? Open arms? Another daddy for Noah?

I opened the baby bag and pulled out wipes, cleaning Noah up and checking his diaper, and that gave me time to think, even if Arvy was standing by the door with his boots on and his jacket already zipped. Talk about eager.

I prevaricated as much as I could, determined to make the right decision, and then I realized I was making no decision at all. If Stan told me to fuck off, then great, I'd accept that. But Stan had asked me about my feelings, and I'd been honest. At least I thought I'd been honest.

Finally we were in the car and heading to Stan's place, and Noah was awake and burbling away. He'd need feeding soon, but I was damn lucky to have a baby who didn't seem to care that he was eating and sleeping in all kinds of different places.

We pulled up at the gate and it was locked. Which meant me sneaking in and getting my car wouldn't have worked. Seemed that Arvy knew the number, though, and the gates swung open.

"How many people know his number? Isn't that some kind of security risk?"

Arvy snorted. "First off, he often uses the bus to get home, and secondly what is his jersey number?"

"30." I thought everyone knew that, but he wasn't asking me an actual question.

"See, easy, his gate code is 3030—so predictable."

We pulled up next to my car, and not for the first time did I notice the difference between mine and every other team member's vehicle. Arvy's was one of the most sensible, and even that was an Audi Q7. One day I'd get a new car, one with auto defog and a working radio. Of course, that was way down the list, after actual furniture.

In the time it took for Arvy to turn off the engine and walk to the front door, his enthusiasm for this visit had waned a little. He brushed his hair with his fingers and posed for me.

"You think she'll like this? How do I look?"

"Like a hockey player trying too hard," I deadpanned, because I could, and because it took my mind off what I was doing there. He sent me a look that spoke volumes and muttered a curse word under his breath, then he rang the bell, and the door opened after a short pause.

Galina answered the door, and her eyes went from me to Noah and then to Arvy. She smiled, and Arvy was right; she had a beautiful smile and looked so much like her older brother.

"I'm sorry, Stan is out right now. He's walked to buy ice cream."

Ice cream? I hadn't even known this exclusive neighborhood had shops. I didn't say that, but I wished I had, because there was one of those awkward pauses while Galina and Arvy stared at each other.

"I like your jersey," Arvy said.

She looked down at the standard Railers practice jersey, which hung loose on her. She really needed to get one that wasn't her brother's.

"Thank you?" she said, as a question.

Arvy didn't stop, he just kept on talking. "I could get you one of mine, maybe in a smaller size."

It would have been a funny situation had we not been standing in the cold, with Noah in my arms.

"That would be nice," she said, and startled when I cleared my throat. "Sorry, you shouldn't have the baby out in the cold. Would you like to come in and wait for Stan?"

Arvy was in quicker than I'd ever seen him move, and I followed a little more sedately. Noah was still awake, his eyes wide, and I stood and waited for what was next. Should we take off our coats? Were we staying?

"Can I take your coats? Come into the kitchen—I have coffee, and I can find something for the little one."

Galina reached for Noah, who I swear was flirting, with his best wide eyes, Cupid's bow smile, and a soft, cooing *bah* sound. He twisted his fingers in Galina's hair and tugged, and she just laughed.

I didn't have to be an expert to see Arvy falling in love with her the very second she laughed and held a baby.

It had never been that way for me and Freja, but I can't tell you how many times I'd thought I should try.

We drank our coffee and ate tiny breads with sugar that Galina called *Plyushka*. She took Noah and held his bottle for him, tenderly brushing his curls from his fore-head. The house was warm and still decorated from New Year's, softly lit with candles, and I was relaxing and nearly forgetting the kind of conversation I had to have with Stan.

Arvy was chatting now, talking about hockey and asking questions about Russia, and nerves had given way to smooth conversation. Galina talked with an accent, but her English was so much better than Stan's. When Arvy asked her, she explained that Stan only had time for hockey, and hadn't thought to learn much English until last summer.

"Something changed," she said. "He began to actually listen to people who told him to learn, and he's taking lessons."

I nodded as she explained. Had Stan told her about last summer? Had he mentioned how the Swedish hockey player had used him, or had he called it breaking his heart? And had he started to learn English because of me?

Of course he hadn't, but still, the warmth of associa-tion rested in my chest, and I smiled.

TEN

Stan

_____

M y neighborhood is what is called upper class. Big, expensive homes. Fancy cars. Someday I think I'll buy the biggest American car I can. Maybe a Cadillac. That's the mark of success in America. Big cars. Big houses. Big boats. Big, big, big. Like my ice cream. A big tub of chocolate with marshmallow. Everything here was super-sized, jumbo, enormous.

So different from my childhood home. Yet the sound of children out playing in the snow was the same. Several ran up to me, eyes bright, cheeks red and wet, all with hockey sticks in hand.

"Mr. Stan, will you play with us?" asked Darren, the boy who brings me my daily paper. I glanced up at his house, a sprawling two-story with an attached two-car garage. There in front of the two doors, in the recently plowed drive, sat a net. "I know my dad said we shouldn't bother you because you're busy, but now you're just walking with ice cream."

He made a good point. I smiled down at the boys and girls. "I am happy to play with you."

They cheered. I shoved my tub of ice cream into the bank of snow along the drive, and settled into the net, the pipes resting on my back. Someone brought me an old wooden goalie stick.

"That's all we got," the young lady informed me. "It was my grandfather's."

Yes, I believed it was that old, but I thanked her anyway and got ready to block the rubber ball they were using instead of a puck. That was a mother's touch—that pink rubber ball—I was almost certain. The next forty minutes was spent blocking shots, laughing, and passing on what knowledge I could with my good but not great English.

When it was time for me to go, they all waved and thanked me. I grabbed my ice cream and continued home, feeling like a hundred bucks. No. Wait. It is more than that. A thousand bucks! I was feeling like a thousand bucks all the way home. When I saw that my friend Arvy was there, my high spirits got higher. This was also good. Another way to keep the memory of what had happened in my kitchen with Erik shoved aside. Right now, I would take any kind of distraction to help me not think, because thinking had only made me edgy, upset, and confused beyond help.

I did not expect to see Erik sitting in my living room, smiling over something my sister had said. Damn. How did I do this? Walk past and grunt? Maybe. Yes. That was good.

"Stan, come see this baby," Galina called as I stalked past after grunting. Lucy trotted out from the kitchen, weaving around my legs, meowing for attention. I bent down and picked her up with one hand and continued moving forward. Not once did I look back at Erik or Noah.

Hearing the baby cooing made it hard not to go back. He was a sweet babe.

Lucy made spitting sounds.

"I know you are not football."

I placed her on the counter alongside the tub of ice cream. She gave me a dark look, then sat down to tend to her ruffled fur.

"You will get good food. Meow, meow, meow, meow," I sang like an old commercial for cat food I had seen on YouTube. I like those old commercials. They're funny and have good songs and clever, snappy lines.

"Hey, you got a minute?" Erik. Damn the man. He had caught me singing the "Meow, Meow" song to my cat.

"I'm not sure I have many minutes. Must feed cat." I waved a hand at Lucy, who was licking a personal girl-cat place.

"When you're done feeding the cat, then. Maybe?"

"Maybe." I moved around the kitchen for a few minutes, opening a can of tuna cat food and dumping it into the tiny bowl beside the water dish. Lucy jumped down to the floor and strolled to her dish, smelled the food, and then walked away. Such a cat.

When I glanced up, he hadn't moved from the doorway. Looking too good. He wore jeans well. They fit him good. No baggy droopy pants on Erik. Always nicely fitted, a little snug on his powerful thighs. If he would turn just a bit his ass would be firmly held in soft denim.

"Stanislav, Arvy and I are going to the movies."

I threw a fast look at Galina, who was handing off Noah to his father.

"But I have ice cream," I stammered, because if she left that would mean I'd have to talk to Erik. I wasn't ready for talking. Hand jobs, yes, it seemed, but talking, no. I was a fucking ham as Tennant would say. No. Wait. Ham is when you are upset. What is it when you are scared? Roasted chicken! I was a roasted chicken, by the General. Or Colonel? It was some military chicken man.

"Which we'll have when we get back." She ran over to me, rose to her toes, and kissed my cheek. "Don't wait up. *Proschay!*"

Out she ran, shouting at Arvy to hurry up. Don't wait up? But it was only maybe noon. What movie would last that long? Erik and Noah both looked at me.

"What do you want?" That sounded angry. Was I angry? No. Yes. A little. Not at Noah, though. "I would hold him please?"

"Oh, yeah, sure." Erik came to me and passed over the little boy.

Noah smiled at me, said "Bah!" and slapped me on the nose.

"You want this ice cream put in the freezer?"

"*Da*, yes."

"I know what 'Da' means," he said offhandedly. A memory of Helsinki appeared unbidden inside my head. Erik spread out over me, riding me as I cried out "*Da, da, da,*" until I blew apart buried deep inside him. I placed the child on my hip and left the kitchen in a hurry.

"Stan, we need to talk."

I sat on the couch, placed Noah on my thighs, and stared at the child. His cheeks were round, his mouth a little bow, and his eyes big and green, like his father's.

"Make talk. I listen."

I heard him exhale. Noah reached for my nose. He seemed to like it. It was a good nose. Long but very Russian. A proud nose.

Erik sat on the other end of the couch. "I want to make sure you understand everything. Where I'm coming from."

"From Sweden, this I know."

Noah burbled and drooled down the front of his little yellow sweater. I made a face at him and got another smile.

"No, I mean my reasoning."

I threw him a fast look. He seemed quite intent on this for some reason. I nodded at him, then went back to his son, who did not make me feel like my stomach was being pulled out through my left ear.

"You leave me. Get married. Have Noah."

"Yeah, that's the high spots, but it's not that simple." He blew out another breath. "Stan, last summer was… Helsinki meant so much to me."

"Yes, so much you go off and marry woman. That is so much meaning?" I snapped. Noah's smile faded at my sharp tone. "Sorry, little bunny," I cooed, and the pout went away.

"I married her because I wanted to do the right thing. The adult thing. You understand that, right? Being responsible?"

"I do responsible much. Bring mother over maybe soon. I make responsible for her," I said, in an even tone so not to upset Noah. I felt like I had a thousand shouts locked inside me. Each one had to be tamed so not to scare the precious one on my lap. "You marry woman after saying love me. I see pictures on Instabook."

"Instagram," he said softly. I nodded. "Right, well, I know you saw them. I was trying, Stan. Trying to be the father that Noah needed. Kids deserve a family."

"Family made of lies? Or was words for me lies?"

That question made him leave the sofa. Erik paced the room, pushing his fingers through his curls, working on how to say what he needed to say in simple words for me.

"See you and Freja broke me," I interjected into his circling laps of the couch.

He stopped pacing then, his hands dropping to his sides, and closed his eyes as if in pain. If he was, good. I wanted him pained. He should suffer as I had.

"I never wanted to hurt you but...I did what I had to do to make sure that Noah could be mine forever. I manned up. I left behind the most important person in the world at that time—the man I'd fallen crazy in love with—to be a dad."

Noah tugged on my nose as I stared openly at his father. "You love me yet?"

"I never stopped. Ever." He rushed around the sofa and sat beside me, his gaze now hopeful and green. Oh, so green. Like the forests of my native country. "She was talking abortion. I said if she kept him that he would stay with me. Be mine. I didn't love her, but we married so it was official, that is all." He reached out to run a hand over his son's bouncy yellow curls. Noah made happy baby noises for his papa. The ice inside me, I think it started to melt a little.

"Now what is right for him?"

"I don't know." Erik fell back against the cushion. "I'm working my ass off to make a new life for him and me. It's the hardest thing I've ever done."

"Being good papa is hard." I had to give him that. Raising a child alone was nothing but work and worry, my mother would say.

"Yeah, it is, but all the hard stuff is worth it when he smiles at me."

Okay, yes, I could see that. Noah's smile made me feel bright inside, like someone had turned a beacon on in my chest. The light flowed out of me back to him. It was good and happy. And he smelled like baby shampoo, which made me feel brighter.

"Stan, you do understand why I did what I did now, right?"

My gaze stayed on the happy baby. "Yes, I understand."

Erik sighed as if I had taken the weight of the world off his shoulders.

""Thank god. Are you still mad? I totally understand that you were hurt and that it will take time to get over that, if you even can. I'd like to maybe be friends someday."

I bounced the baby to give myself time to think. Could I be friends with him? Did I want that, or did I want more? Or less? Smart people would tell me to accept his truths and then let him go live his life. Be polite in the dressing room, talk nicely to the press, and move on. Smart people would tell me that putting aside a hot summer of lust to work on a new and maybe better relationship in the future would make me as smart as they were. Galina would be one of those smart people. She never rushed into love as I had. My sister was flat-headed. No. Wait. That's not right. Flat-headed would be like Herman Munster. I liked that show too.

"Stan?"

"I will take thinking time," I informed him, then hugged his son tight to my chest. The boy snuggled into me. The light inside me glowed a little brighter.

"Really? Okay, that's cool." His rough chuckle pulled my attention from cuddling with Noah. "I thought you were going to beat me up and throw my body into the Volga."

"Volga no flow in Pennsylvania. I throw body into Sus-key-hand-ah."

Erik laughed again. "Susquehanna," he corrected.

"Yes, that river." Noah stopped moving so much. "Is he going asleep?"

Erik leaned around me, close to me, and peered around his son's head. "Yeah, I think he's finally giving up."

My gaze lingered on Erik's mouth, the way it moved when he talked. I liked the way his mouth moved.

"I'd take him home, but Arvy has my car seat in his car and he kind of..." He made a motion with his hand to indicate something moving. "I'll just go into one of the other rooms and lay down with him so you don't have to have my face in yours." He started to rise.

"Sit."

He sat.

"I will hold Noah for nap. We sit and watch TV Land. There is marathon for Andy Griffith and Opie."

"You sure?"

"Yes. Your face is fine while I have thinking time."

Erik found the remote, sat down beside me, his hip next to mine, and turned on the TV. I whistled softly to the theme song, Noah sleeping on my chest, and used up two hours of thinking time not thinking at all, just feeling. And the feelings were toasty warm like one of Aunt Bee's buttermilk pies.

A WEEK later we were in Minnesota and things were not going well. We were in the middle of a losing streak that was filling all our heads with self-defeating thoughts. Despite what our coach and captain said, we couldn't seem to find our stride, and this game against the Wild was not helping build confidence.

They'd come out strong and scored within forty

seconds of the opening face-off. I hate goals so early like that. They shake up the team and prevent me from slipping into the mindset needed to remain focused. Think of it as being awoken gently by soft sounds of nature that lull you into the day or having someone blow a foghorn beside your head to wake you.

I hate foghorn games. After that initial goal, I felt off. The team fell into a shocked kind of dejection that found us scrabbling to keep up with the other team. The forwards were sloppy, the defense spotty. That opened gaping holes in front of my net that left me open and vulnerable, especially to deflections. After two more pucks snuck past me I began to get mad. Mad at myself, mad at the team for not scoring or protecting my crease, and mad at the coaching staff for not shuffling lines to find something that might work.

When the first period ended, I slammed off the ice and into the away dressing room, so mad I could shit. No. Wait. Spit. So mad I could spit.

"Stan, I am so sorry about the last deflection," Dieter was saying behind me as we clumped into the dressing room. "That was totally on me. I should have covered my man better."

"Dude, we're all to blame. Not Stan. No way you get the blame for this," Tennant chimed in.

"My job to stop pucks." Pushing around them, I found my spot in the corner. I sat down, buried my face in my palms, and worked on breathing exercises. One long breath in, fill the lungs, then slowly exhale until the lungs were empty.

No one spoke to me. They barely looked in my direction. Coach talked about tightening up in the corners and finding our forecheck. He pointed out that the backup goalie for the Wild had only had to block three shots in twenty minutes of hockey, while I had been barraged with seventeen. Also, he was not happy about the slashing calls. Overall, Coach was quietly mad about everything and wanted us to pull our heads out of our asses.

The second period was better. Arvy scored a goal, and that swung momentum to us for several shifts. Minnesota got a tripping call and we went on the power play. Tennant found the back of the net on a slap-shot that bounced off the pipes behind the Wild goalie. I reached back to stroke the pipes and ask them to be nice to me even though they were Minnesota pipes and not Harrisburg pipes.

Just when we were starting to really feel the surge of confidence, one stupid move in front of me by Adler Lock-hart set off a string of bad luck. Adler got mad and cross-checked one of the Wild forwards who was screening me. It was a stupid thing to do. He knew it. I knew it. Everyone there knew it. Once he was sitting in the penalty box, our penalty kill unit came out and the wheels started coming off the cart.

The Wild converged on my net. Shots came in so fast I was working on instinct to keep them out of the net. After a flurry that lasted over a minute, Tennant finally managed to clear the puck to other end of the ice. Our side changed out one PK line for another. I caught my breath and tried to lock on to the Minnesota forward charging over the blue line with the puck. Assuming he would slip around our defense, I crouched down, and then he drew back for a slap shot. The puck was a black blur.

It hit Arvy right in the leg, and down he went. This was nothing unusual. Blocked slap shots happen often. The pain is intense but fades after several minutes, leaving a big bruise and swelling. Arvy pushed up to his skates, his face a mask of agony, and pushed along on one skate. The Wild were buzzing like African bees—there was no way he could leave the ice—and so he played on until Adler was released from the penalty box. The puck was iced, and Arvy barely made it to the bench. As soon as he was through the door, the head athletic trainer was on him, helping him down the tunnel to the locker room. A TV timeout occurred.

I skated to the bench, got fresh water in my bottle, and made eye contact with Erik. We'd not spoken much over the past week. He was giving me room to think. It was a funny situation we were in now, and I wasn't sure how much longer we could keep it up. Everyone looked deeply worried about our injured teammate.

"You good, Stan?" I nodded at my coach, took my water bottle from a trainer, and went back to my crease.

"Minnesota pipes," I murmured as the game was about to start again. "I am good man. Strong Russian. Love pipes much. Be good to me."

I rubbed them as one would a lover's bare thigh. Then I turned to face the ice.

The Minnesota pipes didn't love me like my home pipes did. They were callous and uncaring. They deflected a shot into the net behind me and did not send any away. When the game was over, I spun on my skates and flipped the net and the evil Minnesota pipes over. Then I whipped them with my stick until the stick shattered.

The locker room was quiet as a church. We were all worried about Arvy. He'd been taken to the nearby hospital for X-rays of his right leg. The ride back to the hotel was dismal. There was no laughter or teasing on the bus. Just big, silent men humped up in their seats. When we got to our lodgings, everyone scattered, going to their rooms to sulk or think. Erik was in front of me in the elevator. I stood behind him, inhaling the scent of his shampoo while enjoying the way gold curls danced on the nape of his neck.

When we filed out on the fourth floor, I followed him to his room, which was the opposite direction of mine. He tossed me several curious looks as we walked down the nicely carpeted corridor.

"Is there something you want?" he asked as he scanned his card. The lock beeped and the door opened.

I shoved him inside, slammed the door shut, and rounded on him. "You. I want you."

ELEVEN

Erik

I hit the wall with as much force as being pushed into the boards by the biggest D-man in the league, and my breath left me in a whoosh.

"Stan—"

He gripped my hair tight, twisting his fingers into my curls, and yanked me toward him for a kiss. I was off balance, gripping him hard to stand upright, and he pulled my hair to get me to tilt my head, devouring my neck with kisses and bites that I knew could leave marks.

"Your fault," he muttered between kisses, and held me even tighter, as if he wanted to hurt me, as if it was the only way he could get off, using anger and pain.

A loud thump echoed in the room and I realized it was the door.

"Erik, you okay in there, man?"

The captain right outside my room. Stan released his hold on me, and I scrambled to stay upright before catching the material of his jacket. He looked stricken, as if someone had thrown an entire bucket of water over him, cooling his furious passion.

"I'm good," I called. "Knocked into the table."

Stan took another step away, the tightness in his expression slowly turning to remorse. He was going to leave—I could see the panic in his eyes, and then the sadness.

"Jesus," Connor called, "mind your legs. I don't want anyone else in the hospital tonight."

I winced at that, and the fact that Stan was even further away from me, practically in the freaking bathroom. I was so hard; Stan knew every button to press, every word and gesture, pushing me around and making me feel every time. Being shoved around every so often, Stan using his weight and strength against me...fuck, it was the best thing about whatever toxic mess we had going between us.

"Sorry, Captain," I called out. "Night."

There was some muttering from outside the door, more words, but I wasn't really listening. All I knew was that the voice was receding and that I'd been reminded that Connor was in the room next to mine.

Stan was pressed right up against the wall between the bedroom and the bathroom, his palms flat to the wall, his eyes wide. He looked scared. Was he scared of me? Or us? Or being found out? It was probably losing control; Stan didn't lose control very often. He'd run now. I knew it as I knew my own name. His stupid head would be spinning this and making it a terrible thing, when fuck, it could be the best thing ever to happen to us.

I went with my instincts, prowling toward him, and he shook his head a little.

Nope. I wasn't having this. He'd started something that he clearly needed, and this was happening. One way or another, I was getting him inside me tonight. When only inches separated us, I really thought he would run, and I tensed, but he didn't even move. I shrugged off my jacket and flung it toward the chair, not even caring that it might well end up on the floor. And then I loosened my tie and unbuttoned my shirt, taking the whole thing off in one move. That made him flinch, and he leaned to one side, as if readying himself to run. My pants would have to stay on; I couldn't take the chance that he'd sidestep me, even if my cock was so hard that I just wanted it out.

I reached for his hand, and he let me take it, then I went to my knees in a smooth move, right in front of him.

"*Nyet*," he murmured, but I wasn't having any no's tonight. He was fucking me, and I was showing him the way. I took his hand and rested it on my head, carding it through my hair, and instinctively he gripped my curls. I released my hold and leaned forward, pressing my mouth against his cock hidden in his pants. He was as hard as steel, and I kissed him through the fabric and he groaned. Unzipping him was easy, all while kissing and nuzzling him, but still his hands didn't move in my hair, they stayed still; he was striving for complete control, but I knew one way to get his resolve to crack.

I pulled down his pants, his underwear, and nuzzled him again. The heat of him against my skin was another reminder of better times. Reflexively, he dug into my hair a little, not as hard as he needed, not as hard as I liked, but enough to know I was getting to him. His jersey boxers were just under his balls, and I licked and sucked on every part I could reach, then took the tip of him into my mouth. I sucked, just on that end, the weight of him heavy on my tongue, and then as his fingers flexed in my hair I slid my lips forward, taking more of him into my mouth. So deep I nearly gagged before sliding back up. I let him go, looked up at him, just as I knew he wanted me to, how he loved me to, with his fingers in my hair and me on my knees. This was his kryptonite.

"*Eton piz`dets*," he said, his voice hoarse. *This is fucked up.* There was nothing fucked up about me and Stan together. Nothing wrong with *us*.

"Stan," I said, my words a command and a plea.

"*Nyet*," he said, but this time the word was accompanied by him tightening his hold on my hair. He was done, and he knew it, and I knew it, and it was powerful.

I swallowed him down, and he held me. With his fingers twisted in my hair, he held me there, then loosened them enough for me to move back a little and breathe. I went limp in his hold and silently begged to be used.

Cursing in a mix of Russian and English, he fucked my mouth, held me tight, and I gripped his ass, seeking balance and needing to feel him. He was going to lose it soon, I could tell—the way his hips stuttered, the way language of any sort vanished and he was just moaning. When he let me back a little, I put my cards on the table between breaths.

"Inside me," I begged, and he cursed and yanked me up at the same time, and fuck, I was so hard I was scared I'd lose it in my pants. We scrambled to get me out of the remainder of my clothes and to get him naked. Gloriously naked, fucking hot, and erect, and rooting around in my bag for something to use as lube. When he pulled out the bottle and condoms, he looked at them momentarily, and it must have dawned on him that I'd brought them for a reason, but he couldn't know that I'd had them on me ever since he'd shoved his Russian ass back into my life.

I wouldn't be the one to start things, but fuck, I was going to be ready.

"On bed," he commanded, as loudly as he could and still whisper, and I did as I was told, on all fours, needing him now. This wasn't kissing and flowery words; this was a connection at the deepest, hardest level. He covered himself, pressed fingers into me, and then he was inside me, pausing until my body let him in, and then I was full. He moved against me like that, my cock hanging, rubbing the covers. I needed more, but right then I wanted to be on that edge where the need built and where I demanded more.

He pushed hard, deep, and then slowly pulled back, fucked into me again, and I splayed my hands, giving myself balance to rock against him. He reached around me, and I thought this was it, that he would close his hands around my cock and I could finally come with him after all this time. But all he did was wrap his arms around me, pull me up, his hands moving to my chest and steadying me. The angle, my back to his front, meant he could go deeper, and his fingers pulled and twisted my nipples until I was nothing but sensation. He whispered things in my ear, heated Russian, words he'd taught me.

I'm fucking you. I want you. I love your cock. I'm fucking you.

I'm fucking you.

"Please," I begged. I needed his hands on me, but all he did was fuck me hard and bite my neck and pull on my nipples, and I was going to come. He used one of his hands in my hair, twisted me to kiss me, and I was so close. "Please…" I begged into the kisses.

"I'm get you there," he whispered, and then he was coming, stiffening beneath me, fucking up into me, and his hand was on my cock, and it took two strokes, no more, and I was coating his fingers and forcing my hand into my mouth to stop myself shouting. For the longest time, he held me, until he had softened enough to pull out. He disposed of the condom. I lay down on the bed, totally boneless, my nipples aching, my cock spent, exhaustion flooding me.

"Why you have these?" Stan asked softly, and I turned my head to see the condoms and lube. Stan looked deadly serious.

"For you," I murmured, "always for you."

He curled his fingers in my hair, but softly, massaging my scalp, and I was taken back to our time in Helsinki, when he would spend hours playing with my hair after we'd made love. Then his hand was gone, and I was tired and closed my eyes.

When I woke up, to a clock that showed four a.m., Stan was gone.

And my heart ached for the loss.

MY CELL WOKE me at six a.m., this time with a call from Amy, who wanted to know where Noah's health records were. She needed them to check up on inoculations, and I explained they were in the third box from the bottom in the pile in my room. She sent me a quick LOL.

That was a running joke between me and her, the fact that I'd never actually unpacked, choosing instead to throw a cover over the boxes and pretend the unpacked mess was a cupboard or something. It wasn't as if we were staying in that apartment anyway; it was an emergency let, and I needed to find somewhere to stay for real. Maybe I should take the team up on what they'd offered, or yeah, get some money out of them at least. I made a mental note to search for finances, and sent a quick text to my agent, Sven Haalsen, whose job it was to keep on top of salaries.

Amy texted me to say she'd found the records and that I needed to unpack.

Yeah, yeah, whatever.

I didn't text that, but I wasn't staying in that place, and

I wouldn't unpack until I felt more settled than I did right then.

When you're traded, when you get the call, you never really expect to stay where you're sent. There are a million ways to fuck up. I could have been the best in my AHL team but been crap coming up to the NHL. The Railers could have sent me packing, and that would have been it, I would have been out of the NHL, back down to the AHL, and god knew if the Rush would have kept me.

Next thing I knew I'd have been in Canada, or LA, or Florida.

But somehow, I was doing okay. My line had clicked, Charlie, Toly and I were giving a solid, respectable fourth line showing, and I wanted to stay.

With the team.

In Penn.

With Stan.

Make a home, find a proper place for me and Noah.

A text came in from Sven. Money had been released, I didn't need to worry, and could I make sure that I did well enough to get another couple of years on the Railers, as he liked them.

I'll try, I thought, *even if it does mean coming to some kind of agreement with Stan.*

I showered and dressed, knowing that whatever time it was I would find someone up and ready to show me to coffee. Connor was the one I spotted first in the hotel's twenty-four-hour coffee shop, surrounded by the remnants of a breakfast burrito and two coffees. He looked as he hadn't slept, and immediately my thoughts went to Arvy.

"Shit," I said, and slid into the seat opposite him and asked about Arvy. "Is it that bad?"

Connor looked at me—focused right on me, despite the bloodshot eyes. "You tell me," he said cryptically.

Me? I hadn't heard anything about Arvy that morning. Had I missed a text? I checked my phone, but there was nothing.

"Was there a message in some kind of group chat? I'm not in a team group." I tried not to let that hurt—after all, I was new on the Railers, and maybe they didn't even have a group chat. If they did, then Ten would be in charge of it, no doubt.

Connor leaned forward and passed me his cell, which I turned to face me. There was a notepad app open and some words on it. "You want to translate this that I heard through my freaking wall when I was trying to sleep?"

The words made no sense to read, and then I sounded the words out phonetically, and it hit me. Connor in the next room. Connor hearing Stan saying he was fucking me, and to *suck him down*. Connor writing down the words he'd heard.

"Shit," was all I said.

Connor crossed his hands on the table and banged his head on them, twice, three times. I was worried our captain was going to give himself a concussion. He mumbled something that sounded suspiciously like the words "odd one out" and "fuck my life", but I didn't like to ask.

Connor lifted his head, "Just…jeez…do me a favor…"

"Anything," I said immediately

"I'm already down a defenseman—don't fuck up Stan's game over this shit."

Wow, that was honest and direct and made me acutely aware of my place on the team. I guessed if it was Stan or me, then it would be the fourth line winger who was out of a job.

So much for dreams of putting down roots.

"You're saying we can't—"

"I'm saying it's your life, but next time keep the noise down, and don't mess with Stan's head. He's a good guy."

So am I, I thought, but I didn't say it out loud.

"Please don't tell anyone," I said softly, recalling Stan's fear of exposure and word getting back to anyone around his mom in Russia.

"I won't," he said, and he looked tired, so I decided to change the subject.

"How is Arvy?"

Connor sighed heavily. "He's comfortable."

That didn't sound good; if anything it sounded like a death sentence for a hockey player.

"Is he coming back with us now?"

"Doc Roberts is staying with him, and they'll be going back to Harrisburg."

Which meant he wouldn't be flying with us for our next away game in Toronto.

Silence. He stared at me, and I felt as uncomfortable as if a million fire ants were crawling over me.

"Stan and I," I began.

Connor held up a hand. "We have an inclusive team, you know that, but we need Stan, okay?"

There they were again—the damning words that I was replaceable—but it seemed as though Connor wanted to continue.

"And Erik, you're the best fourth line winger in the AHL. The Rush were lucky to get you, we're lucky to have you plugging away for us. Don't fuck it up."

"Yes, Captain."

Connor collected his stuff and left without asking anything else, and for a while I sat there staring into nothing, aware of the team coming in and out of the breakfast room. Someone brought me coffee, someone else placed a plate of bacon in front of me. I must have looked spaced-out. I was alternating between pride at Connor's words and terror of what I might do to Stan.

At this point in the story of Erik and Stan, I could back away. I had a baby, I needed to find a place to live, and Stan was likely still on a strong hating-me kick. But he didn't have to be. Right?

The Erik/Stan story didn't have to end now. I didn't have to back away; I could work at this, and we could get back what we'd lost.

So now I was standing at the crossroads and unsure which way to go when Stan slipped into the chair opposite me.

"Not do bad thinks," he said.

"Okay," I agreed, even though I didn't know what the hell he meant—bad thoughts or something, I guessed.

"Focus Leafs," he added. "Not bad game for Leafs."

"You want to focus on the game." My heart stopped, because he was echoing what Connor had said and, hell, he was right. This was about the team, not some stupid kid like me who could cause problems.

He nodded and sat back, crossing his arms over his chest. "And on us," he added, and he half smiled.

Hope swelled in my chest.

TWELVE

Stan

———

Sitting across from Erik that morning with the cold winter sun touching his golden hair, I had no idea how or what "focusing on us" meant, but I knew that it was as vital to me as breathing. I could see the warmth of promise light up his beautiful jade eyes, and it filled my breast with potential as well. How to act on it was just not clear.

We tried to be professional on the road, because for me, coming out big was not going to happen. My mother still lived in Leskovo, which sat perhaps five miles from the border of Chechnya. Terrible things were going on in the Chechen Republic—purges of gay men, deaths and murders. If word spread of her son being gay…

So, no, there would be no splashy "pressers" for Layton Foxx to organize for Erik and me. Not until my mother was safely in America. Then perhaps we could simply be. As much as I respected and admired Tennant and Coach Madsen for being brave and facing the fire, I could not, nor would ever be so happy for the attention. I wasn't sure how Erik would feel about this, and I had yet to talk to him about it, for private time was strictly limited.

On the road, we slipped into playing that we were friends only. Erik and I talked hockey on the bus, on the plane, during scrimmages and practice, but at night we went to our rooms alone. I longed to go to him and hold him, merge my body with his, talk about things that held meaning for us, but in a hotel filled with ears and eyes, no, that could not be. Our captain already knew of our secret according to Erik. There could be no others discovering our new romance…if one could call it a romance. It was a most unsettling time, but we struggled through that long road trip, picking up three wins to help even out the losses on the road.

My house, my cat, and my sister were waiting for me when I arrived home at the end of January, but not for long.

"I'm going to visit Arvy today," she informed me as she swept through the living room, pulling on a coat.

"But I have come just home," I said, my cat draped around my neck, making claw marks in my blue suit jacket.

"Yes, and you are so handsome. I'll be at his place. Text me if you need anything. Happy homecoming, big brother!" She ran over, kissed my cheek, and raced off. Why would she run off when I had so much I needed to talk to her about? She was the only person who knew I was gay, and so I'd held everything inside about Erik and me to tell her. Did a broken leg outweigh a brother who had deep secrets to confide? What did she care about Arvy? They barely knew each other.

Lucy purred into my ear. "Yes, pretty one, you are always here for me."

I reached up to scratch her soft head, then carried my bags to my room. She leaped from my shoulder onto the bed and curled up on her pillow. I looked around my bedroom. It was so big, so nicely decorated, and so empty. Sharing this night with Lucy was not what I had wanted at all, not that she was not a loving pussy-cat. She was. And she adored me. I wanted human contact, though. Someone to talk to who would understand. Someone like Galina, or Mama. Or Erik…

As soon as I thought of him, my body reacted with heat and yearning. So much yearning that I rushed to change into jeans and a thick fleece sweatshirt. I pressed a kiss to Lucy's head and left her to nap, my blood hot in my veins. I jogged to the nearest bus stop, climbed into a warm city bus, and pulled out my phone to play music and double check his address as he had entered it into my phone. I rode to his apartment building on Derry Street. It was a big one, with perhaps ten floors. I studied the big sign with the address to be sure I was in the right place. Puzzled about why he would live in a rather rundown building when he played professional hockey, I went inside and rode to the eighth floor, my earbuds resting on my neck so that I could hear Elvis singing sweet romance songs.

The elevator opened onto a long corridor. I exited and went in search of apartment 8D, which was one door past a home with loud children.

The tiny girl who pulled the door open gawked up at me, her eyes going wide.

"I am Stanislav. I have business with Erik Gun—"

The door slammed in my face. I had never had a door closed on me before. I looked up and down the long hallway and lifted my hand to knock again. The door flew open, and Erik smiled up at me, his cheeks a soft pink.

"Stan, sorry, that's Amy, my nanny. She thought you were Russian mafia coming after me and kind of got spooked." I looked over his head at the nanny clutching young Noah to her breast.

"Ah, no, I no Russian mafia," I said to soothe the skittish young thing. "I am Russian goalie. No make Erik dead with shoes of cement."

"She watches too many crime dramas," Erik whispered, then stepped back so I could enter his house.

"Ah, shoot 'em ups," I mumbled as I ducked to avoid a forehead injury. "Chuck Connors is big rifleman."

"No, not Westerns, crime dramas like… It's not important. This is a surprise—seeing you here, I mean."

I stood in the center of his living room in my thick woolen peacoat, looking at boxes hidden under sheets, wondering what this was.

"Is this new Swedish table?" I asked, with a wave at the boxes under the covers.

Erik ran his hand over his hair, the curls bouncing back as soon as his fingers cleared them. I wanted to do that. Needed to do that. Yearned to do that. Ah, the yearning was back now. Loud and violently roaring like a Siberian tiger, it clawed at my insides.

"I just haven't unpacked yet. Waiting for the other shoe to drop, you know?"

"I no make cement shoes. I say this time before this time."

The nanny giggled. Noah giggled. Erik snorted. I had no clue what was so damn funny. "Yeah, I know. Listen, I was just about to get lunch. You maybe want to stay?"

The nanny handed Noah to his father, then ducked around me, still looking quite reserved. I scare tiny women like this all the time. Sometimes tiny men too. It's the curse of being a tall, stoic Russian.

"I can stay and help," the nanny said as she pulled on a

pink coat. Erik waved her off. "Okay, well, I'll see you in two days. Welcome home, Mr. G. And, uh, Stan."

"Safe trips to home," I said, and smiled as bigly as I could. No. Wait. Is bigly right word? Yes, it must be, as I heard the President use it. She nodded, then hurried out the door. "Girl is good nanny?"

"Oh yeah, she's great. The road trips are hard on her—you know, being here for weeks on end."

"I hold pretty Noah, please?" I held out my hands. Erik smiled and handed over his son. Noah squealed and instantly grabbed my nose. "He likes nose."

"It's a nice nose. Noble, you know. Like the nose of a Czar."

My gaze met Erik's. The yearning doubled. "No Czar in family. Peasants only. Strong, hard work, steady."

"That sounds just like you." He turned before I could read more in his gaze.

I followed him into a tiny kitchen. This room, too, was barren of homey touches, but was more unpacked than the living room.

"You can put him in his high chair," Erik said over his shoulder as he worked on smashing up soft pears with a fork. I got the boy in his seat, put the tray on, and tied a big plastic bib with a purple penguin around his neck.

"Bah!" Noah said, and smacked his tray with his palms.

"Hold your horses," his dad replied with good humor.

I sat on a chair with weak-looking metal legs and watched Erik getting food ready for Noah. He moved with knowledge of what he was doing, his body language saying he had done this many times and was confident. I enjoyed the dialog between him and Noah, soft and playful. He loved his beautiful son so much.

"So, now that he's got his lunch, what do you want?"

he asked as he wiped up the counter where he'd prepared fresh fruit and oatmeal cereal for his boy.

"You."

Erik looked at me over a broad shoulder. Fire danced in his eyes. "Maybe during nap time?"

"Yes, nap time is good."

He made us sandwiches, thick, with tuna salad and lettuce. We had cheesy potato chips and root beer. Noah ate well but sloppily, tossing his spoon to the floor, the table, my lap, and his father's chest.

"Did you hear the rumors that we're going after Max Van Hellren from Washington?" Erik asked as we worked on our food.

"For Arvy, yes. I hear on Facebook chat group we sign last night."

"Oh. I'm not in any of the team groups."

"Why you no in groups?"

He crinkled his nose. "No one wants me there, I guess?"

"Pah, stupid. I want you in group. I add. Make you Pokémon group too." I pulled out my phone and found Facebook with ease. Erik protested, but in the end, he was in both groups. "There, you play Pokémon now."

"I don't do Pokémon," he said while wiping his sleepy son's face with a warm, damp washcloth.

"Is easy as peasy. I teach," I said as he scrubbed at the boy's cheeks. "You get balls. Go out. Look for Pokémon. Throw ball. Catch Pokémon. Train big. Beat other trainers. Win games! See. Easy as peasy. Must get tattoo to be member of club."

Erik chuckled. "Oh, so that's what your ink work is. As long as it's easy as peasy, then I guess I'll be okay." He removed the tray from the high chair and lifted his baby into his arms. "I'm going to tuck him in."

"I give goodnight kiss maybe please?"

Erik nodded.

I stood up and pressed a kiss to Noah's sweet curls. "Happy dreams, little rabbit," I whispered to him, then moved back to give Erik room to get around me.

For some reason, I followed him through the small apartment. He laid the sleepy baby in his crib, pulled a fluffy yellow quilt up over the boy, and tugged the blinds shut. Noah never made a sound, just dropped off like an angel.

Erik walked to the doorway that I was blocking. "You are good father," I told him, my voice as soft as Noah's tiny breaths.

"I'm trying."

I took him by the wrist and led him out of the baby's room. He closed the door, then flattened his back to the wall. I took his other arm and lifted both hands over his head. He wet his lips as his pupils grew fat with desire.

"Seeing you with him makes me want you much more," I whispered so not to wake Noah. Erik groaned and went to his toes, trying to put his mouth on mine. I turned from the kiss and buried my face in his neck instead, keeping his hands high over his head. "I think of nothing but this. You. Me. Making hot fucking." I chewed on his throat, pulling long, low moans of pleasure from him. Each nip got me a shudder, each mark on his pale skin a rolling keen that made my already hard cock throb strongly. "I would have you in my mouth. Come hard. Keep your hands up there." I pressed the backs of his hands to the wall to emphasize what I wished.

"Yes, okay, yes." He panted and writhed, his hip bone grinding into mine. "Kiss me."

I was happy to do that. His response to my lips on his was explosive. His tongue darted out to slide over mine. He kissed so well, so fervently, that I simply held him in place and tasted of him for a long time. We rocked against each other, stiff pricks teasing and rubbing to the point of madness.

"Stay hands here," I grunted, then went to my knees, the thin carpet not providing much padding, but who cared? Erik was where he wanted to be, and so was I.

I freed his cock, leaving his pants up and just pulling out his prick. I fell on it, taking him down my throat. His ass punched away from the wall. Hands on his tight ass, I set the pace. Erik was always compliant, eager to please, to be fucked and sucked. We were the perfect fit, as I liked to have lovers who did my bidding in bed. Allowed me to love them strongly yet tenderly.

My fingers kneaded his ass cheeks through thin denim. His nails worked the plasterboard when I paid special attention to the underside of his cock, rubbing it with my tongue as I massaged his buttocks.

"Fuck, I'm close," he whimpered.

I took him in hand and squeezed the base of his cock, hard. His head flew back, slamming against the wall. His orgasm hit him like a truck, buckling his knees and yanking erotic sounds from him. He shot on my cheek and shoulder, his cock pulsing as I milked him with long, eager strokes.

I pushed to my feet, and he was all over me. Kissing me, lapping at my neck and jaw, murmuring how he wanted more, needed more, would love more. We stumbled into the bedroom to find the condoms and lube. The ones he kept for me, always for me. Clothes flew to the floor. Erik lay on the bed, his legs held to his chest, his tight hole on display for me.

Seeing him like that made me short of breath and half mad with need. I covered my cock with latex and walked to him, the lube in my hand, my gaze settled on his puckered entrance.

I flipped the lid open and squeezed. Clear slick ran over his balls and ass, then onto the cover under him. Using the edge of the bed to rest my knees on, I grabbed his legs and pulled him to me, dropping down into a half-crouch, so that the head of my cock penetrated him when his ass reached the edge of the bed. The sight of his ass swallowing my cock pushed me into another world. A place of pure sexual pleasure.

"Come up," I snarled. I thrust hard to bury myself in him, then bent over to grab him up off the bed. His eyes widened for a second, then slowly fluttered shut. He wrapped his arms around my neck and his legs circled me. I stood up. Erik slithered down further still. He whimpered. "Too much?" I asked, then turned, the wall my goal.

"No, fuck no, never too much," he ground out. Then his shoulders and back met the wall with a powerful slap. "Ah! Oh, Stan."

"Tell me again is for me only me." I pumped upward, and his body tightened around me, pulling at me, urging me deeper. "Tell me love is only for me. Tell me, Erik. Please tell me."

"For you. Always for you. Love is…fuck, I can't… talk right with you…so fucking deep."

I chuckled at his stuttering laughter, then fucked him like he was the last fuck I would ever have. Erik held on tight, the perfect bottom, hot for my prick, and expressive. He called my name, dug at my shoulders and neck, and rolled his hips down when I thrust up.

Words fell out of me, but I wasn't sure if they were English or Russian. My orgasm hit me from behind, making my legs feel weak and flimsy. I pumped hard into him, going as deep as I could. He whispered and whimpered and begged. His dick was fat and hard now, pressed between us. I felt him reach for it while I was rocking up onto my toes. He came just as I was coming down from the rush. His spunk dotted our chests and stomachs.

My mouth claimed his as his release pulled at him.

"I'm dying," he huffed as he worked his cock, milking it aggressively.

"I am dying too. No, I am dead."

"You've got a pretty stiff dick for a dead man."

"Is Roger Moore this."

"Ah, hell…what?"

"When dead and get hard body."

"Do you mean rigor mortis?" He chuckled.

I thought for a moment, nodded, then laughed as well as I carried him to the bed and laid him across it, falling over him as we sank into the thin mattress.

"Oh, Stan, I fucking missed you." He continued laughing as I removed the used condom and dropped it into a small trash can beside the bed.

"I miss you too. So much. Heart break bad. You never break me again? Please say you no do so." I hadn't meant to get serious and sad, but holding him to me as we smiled and touched was scaring me badly. I'd done this before. Held him like this, talked of love and a future, only to have him walk away. Yes, I know. He had made Noah and was doing what a man should do. Responsibility to family is first always. I understood his choice, and adored his Noah, but still the fear of him ripping me into tiny bits again was strong.

"I promise never to break you again." His reply was manna for my soul. I pressed a soft, tender kiss to his lips, wishing I could speak better so that he knew the depth of feelings I had for him. I pulled him to me, his chest against my side. I ran my fingers through his hair as our bodies cooled, semen drying into a tacky mess. We lingered there for a long time, his eyes closed as he drew small circles on my stomach while I played with his hair.

"Noah will be up soon," he said, his voice as lazy as our limbs.

"I will shower." Dropping a kiss to his bouncy curls, I slid out from under him and got to my feet.

"Oh, hey, can you just wash up in the sink? Amy just did some washing and the water heater is crappy."

"Why you live in peasant housing?" He sat on the edge of the bed, tousled and beautiful and sad suddenly. "You play pro hockey. Make big monies."

"Not so big. I had to give my ex a ton of cash to settle things."

What he was saying made little sense to me. "You give all monies to ex?"

"The majority of it. It's okay, though. I can scrimp a bit for a couple months and then—"

"What is scrimp?"

"Pinch pennies. Like uh, economize. Save money where you can?" He lifted his eyes from the thin carpet to me.

"You make plenty scrimps already."

"No, it's cool. Really. It looks worse than it is because I don't have the time to decorate." I gave him a woolly eyeball. No. Wait. Hairy eyeball. "Seriously, as soon as I get a few days off, I'll unpack and hang some pictures on the wall and it'll look like a palace in here."

I didn't believe him at all, but it was not for me to say how he lived. Still… "You could not scrimps and live with me."

He looked at me as if Baryshnikov were dancing Swan Lake on my head. "Uh, what?"

"Do I not say it in good English? You and Noah could

live with me. Save monies for months then find good house. My house is good. Big. You see house. You like house, yes?"

"Well, sure, it's a beautiful house, but…"

I nodded. "Is beautiful house. Many rooms. And Galina is there for help you nanny with work many weeks yet."

"I can't ask your sister to—"

"There is also cat, Lucy, for making pet for Noah. Big yards. We make fence around yards. Keep Noah safe in summer when outside making baseball games."

The more I thought about it, the more I wanted it. Erik, Noah, Galina. All in my house. Making the house ring with laughter and love. If only I could lure Mama over…

"Stan, I can't just move in with you."

"Why you say no? My house good. Much gooder than this." I waved a hand at the badly painted walls. "I hear people through walls. Smell bad smell in hall. My house has good smell, like Russian food. This place stink like cat box."

"The neighbor has five cats. The smell kind of leeches through the wall," he confessed.

I threw my hands into the air and gave him a look of confusion. "Then why not come to house with air like sweet *tula pryanik*? Russian gingerbread," I added when he looked confused.

"What about the press?"

"We say old friend move in until find new house. No one think gay love. See, work out with good end!"

"I'm not gay, I'm bi."

Ugh. Why was he being such a douche canoe, as Adler would say?

"Yes, I know. You make sex with women too. No one

think gay or bi love then. See, I fix. Come bring things to house."

"No."

"Why no yet?"

"Because I have this in hand. I can take care of my son without handouts. Let me get you a washcloth." He stood up and stalked at me, his jaw firm. I grabbed him as he passed, pulling him tightly to me, then I cupped his cheek, lifting his angry eyes to my face.

"No say bad father." I kissed his unyielding lips. "You are good father. Make much loves for son. Work hard. Strong man. Bring Noah and things here?" I said again. He sighed deeply, then melted into me, leading me away from money talk with his mouth. "Not think dollars." I insisted.

"I'll pay my way." He said and nuzzled my neck.

"We good here, man?"

Something in what I said made him laugh. "Let me guess. Tennant Rowe says that all the time?"

"Yes, good. I learn from Tennant much hip street lingo."

"Maybe I can help teach you some hip street lingo now." He led me into the cramped bathroom down the hall, where we washed each other off while sampling tender kisses. "If you want?"

"I want most much."

THIRTEEN

Erik

"The final paperwork is on its way," my lawyer-from-hell announced as soon as I picked up the phone.

This was the third call I'd had to say that final paperwork was done.

The first time, Freja's lawyers had demanded a section about me having sole responsibility for Noah, financially and in respect to his welfare. I was convinced I'd read a paragraph about that, but no, the lawyers had said it wasn't tight enough.

The second time had been an addition about public knowledge, and some kind of caveat about this that and the other. Who the hell knew? Unless you had degree in law, you would not be able to untangle this for anything.

At the end of the day, I wanted nothing from Freja herself. No money, or status, or acknowledgment.

All I wanted from her was the promise that she would always consider Noah if the occasion arose that it was necessary to speak about him. Oh, and never to want him from me, or want shared custody, and to discuss all visits with me. I had to think about Noah, but when we'd started this journey—when I'd sat down and said I wanted her to carry the baby to term—it had all sounded so simple. I gave money to her charity—a lot of money—she took a sabbatical, Noah would be born, and that would be her part done.

Of course, I'd known that there would be issues over press, but in Sweden our press isn't quite as intrusive as it is in the US, and we'd decided to be brutally honest about our intentions from day one. But in the main, Freja and I were grown-ups, and we didn't need anything on paper to get this done.

Except we did if we wanted this done right.

So much paper, and billable hours, and it had reached the point where I was paranoid that if I signed something wrong, the authorities would swoop in and take Noah. Now, I was certain I wanted every legal angle explored.

"Are we sure?" I asked Lester, my lawyer and my support in this whole thing.

"We had one more codicil concerning Noah when he reaches the age of majority."

"Which is?"

"Which is what?"

"What is Noah's age of majority?"

"Eighteen," Lester said.

Why use the fancy language when he could have just said eighteen to start off with?

"And?" I prompted.

"The codicil, quite right," Lester murmured, as if he wasn't on the phone with me, but talking to himself. I'd met him once, all belly and bluster, but he at least seemed to know what he was doing. "Yes, yes," he said.

Noah bounced in his seat and squished the remainder of his biscuit in his hand, squealing at the excitement of it all. I wished I was in a seat being fed rusks and bananas and generally not having to deal with lawyers.

"What happens when Noah is eighteen?" I prompted again. Frustration must have slipped into my tone, because Lester did this tutting thing that had me rolling my eyes.

"All normal," Lester said. "Financial responsibility, college funds and so on."

Jesus, when was this man actually going to talk to me in plain speech?

"I'm covering all that; I'll be setting up a trust and depositing money into it for a college fund." As soon as I got to the bank to do so.

"Absolutely. Quite so, responsibility and all that."

And then there was silence.

"Lester, when do I get the paperwork?"

"Soon. I'd like to arrange a meeting."

More meetings. More money. I wished I knew more so I could call him on it, but who was I to know what was right and wrong? Maybe divorce and primary-carer status did need me to attend the glass high-rise of Lester, Lester and Merrin, for the ninth time.

"When?"

"Would Friday suit?"

Away game. Shit. "Not a good day for me." I didn't bother explaining the concept of an away game after the last time, when Lester had helpfully suggested that the team could put on a substitute. I hadn't explained that wasn't how it happened, that we didn't have such a thing in hockey and players being called up wasn't easy.

Lester tutted again. "Monday?"

I glanced at the calendar on the wall. Monday was clear. "I could do that."

"Ten forty-five, final papers to sign, Mr. Gunnarsson. Almost there."

Wow, is he actually attempting to reassure me?

Something hit me in the face, and without thinking I wiped at it. Mashed rusk. I ended the call and faced Noah.

At least, somewhere under the milk and biscuit was Noah.

"C'mon, little man, we have cleaning up to do."

I lifted him from his chair and checked the clock. Amy would be here in sixty, Stan not long afterward. I might as well get one last baby bath in at this place, me and Noah and the dribble-splurt of a shitty shower hose. Noah loved water, and he bobbed in my arms in excitement when I turned it on. The water was warm, the pressure pathetic, but he was clean, and I even managed to wash my hands and face. Dressed in the last clothes I'd left out, I stood in the middle of the apartment and tried to feel nostalgic. Inhaling the smell of cat pee, though, I decided that nostalgia was overrated.

Amy arrived at ten, took Noah off me, and then it was just me in the apartment. Me and my boxes of stuff.

Ten thirty, and Stan was at the door. Along with Ten, Jared, Toly, Charlie and Dieter, who all crowded in, making me realize that this small space was *so* not set up for two hockey players, let alone a whole group of them.

"Jeez, this place stinks," Adler announced, and winced when Ten poked him in the side. "Sorry," he mumbled.

"You're right, it does."

"I'm ask help," Stan announced, and picked up the first box. "Quick for cat smell."

I fist-bumped and thanked everyone, and in three trips between us, we had the rented van loaded with mine and Noah's gear. Amy was coming with us as well, but she was moving in seperately.

"You sure you want to share with No-English here?"

Ten quipped, and ducked when Stan went to cuff him around the head.

Jared held him and Stan poked at him, and there was laughter, and fuck, it hit me right then, I really could have friends on this team.

We arrived at Stan's as a convoy of van and cars, all stopping in the circle outside the house. Stan opened one of the garages and gestured inside. "Storing," he explained. "Rest to inside."

Everyone followed my instructions. Some of the boxes could be stored here, but all the baby stuff and clothes needed to go to wherever Stan wanted me to stay.

Which turned out to be what Ten described at the west wing. Less a wing and more a whole side of the house that was empty, there was a room for me, and a connecting nursery. It was the nursery that had me stopping and staring in shock. I had been expecting a simple, plain room, but this had been made into a nursery. A real one. Painted a pale blue, one wall had a huge mural of a family of rabbits having a picnic. The detail was incredible. I could see the sun, and birds, and a hedgehog; the whole picture was a story. There was a fully assembled crib, which put my travel crib to shame, white bedding, and a huge changing table cupboard with shelves above full of stuffed toys.

"You like?" Stan said, and he sounded nervous, as if he thought maybe he'd overstepped, or that I would hate it.

"Wow," was all I said, and I did a full three-sixty to check it all out. This was the room my son deserved; this was what I wanted to give him.

Stan pointed to the mural. "Galina painted," he said.

"I hope it's okay," a soft voice said to the left of me, and I realized Stan's sister Galina was in the room with Noah on her hip.

"You painted that?"

She nodded and wrinkled her nose a little, just as Stan did when he was embarrassed.

"It's gorgeous; you're so talented."

She shrugged, but at least she smiled at me. "And the rest? I asked Amy, and she gave me a list of what Noah needed, but if there is anything missing…"

I hugged her as best I could with Noah there as well. "It's all too much," I said.

"Never much big for little rabbit," Stan said, and held out his arms for Noah, who was happy to be transferred, bumping at Stan's nose with his fist.

The guys all stayed for pizza, but I spent some time in the nursery sorting through clothes instead of joining them for beers. I needed that space, the time to watch my son sleep in his crib and to get used to the idea of living here.

Stan had offered me space, and I desperately needed not to be on my own. I didn't expect monetary help—I wanted to pay my way, and I wanted to be the one who was up with Noah—but I'd seen the main bedroom that was mine, decorated in muted colors. There was a huge, solid oak bed, with pale blue bedding and a lamp on each side. I craved being in there with Stan.

Would it just be my bed? Or would Stan join me? Was it *our* room? Had he clearly told Galina that we were together?

I switched on the baby monitor and went into my room, half closing the door and checking I could hear the soft, muted tones of the mobile as they wound down through the receiver. Then, because I abruptly needed company rather than silence, I made my way downstairs. I couldn't see Dieter or Toly, but Ten and Jared were still there, Ten with his legs up on Jared's lap, laughing at something someone had just said.

"Help me with these, man."

I turned to see who it was, smiling on seeing Arvy limping on crutches but up and mobile. I took the beers from him and hovered by him as he made his way to the sofa, Galina not far behind him, bearing all kinds of snacks on a tray. I set the monitor on the table along with the beers, and sat next to Stan on one of the sofas. There was so much space between us that I couldn't touch him, but that was okay, because everyone would be going home soon.

Galina helped Arvy to sit, then curled up next to him, resting her head on his shoulder. There might have been space between us, but I could have sworn I heard Stan growl.

"Football is bigger money," Stan muttered, and swallowed some beer, coughing when it clearly went down the wrong way. "Not broken hockey man."

Galina frowned at him and laced her fingers with Arvy's. Oh, so this was a thing, then, Galina and Arvy.

"Don't start, Stanislav," Galina said, in plain English.

Stan answered with something that sounded very Russian, and I swear it held a couple of swear words.

Galina stiffened next to Arvy, and she looked angry. I guessed whatever Stan had said hadn't been welcoming Arvy into the bosom of the family. Then she deliberately leaned up, cupped Arvy's face, and kissed him deeply. Arvy flailed a little at first, evidently not expecting that, then he slipped an arm around her and held her close after the kiss. Stan stared at them and tilted his head, and Arvy cleared his throat.

"I love Arvy," Galina announced dramatically.

Arvy's eyes widened and he looked down at her. "You do?" he asked, his voice incredulous.

"I do, I love you," she repeated.

"God, I love you too," he said, and they kissed again.

Stan muttered something. Then, glowering, with his arms crossed over his chest, he made a statement to underline the whole thing. "You hurt, I kill."

Arvy nodded, then hugged Galina even closer. A brown long-haired cat jumped up and settled into the space between me and Stan, pawing at the fabric and then curling up in a contented ball. I reached out to stroke her, assuming this was Lucy, and she purred at me, a small chirrup of noise, before butting my hand. I guessed I'd caught her unawares, but when I looked up, Stan was smiling at me in approval, and I continued to stroke her for a while.

"So, Erik," Ten said, to break the silence. "Now it's just you and Stan who need to be snuggling."

I shot him a look of shock, I know I did, because what he'd just said was…it was a secret… This was… Oh, hell.

Jared sighed and pinched at Ten's jeans. "We weren't going to say anything."

Ten shook his head. "They're with friends, and nothing leaves this room."

Stan looked at me; I could see it in my peripheral vision. At this point, we could do what we did to the world outside—deny what was happening here, deny having anything other than friendship, or we could—

I couldn't even finish that thought, because Stan picked Lucy up, cradled her close, and moved, and the sofa rocked as the big man was by my side with his arm over my shoulders and Lucy on his lap.

"In house, I'm doing," he announced.

Stan rested his chin on my head, just like he used to in Helsinki, hugging me closer. And all I did was lean in, because hell, as I'd learned today, I was with friends.

FOURTEEN

Stan

Two weeks with Erik, Noah, and Galina in my house raced by. I had always dreamed of this kind of life. A huge house with family filling it. My heart was full. Mostly. We still had to get Mama to America. Yes, she was coming. All I had done was bribe her with Noah.

Explaining to her that Erik was living with me as my secret boyfriend had been simple. Trying to make her understand that he had been married to a woman and had a child? That had taken some softly explained facts about bisexuality. While she didn't fully grasp that a person could like both sexes, she was willing to accept it as some confusing fact, like gravity. She didn't understand that either, but she accepted it. Or how a TV worked. Also accepted without deeper knowledge of the exact specifics.

I'd tried to do paperwork for Mama, but had ended up angry and confused by the red tape and indecipherable government language. Erik had encouraged me to turn it over to the team's lawyers, so I'd done that and hoped they would get things dealt with for Mama.

Life was filled with so much happiness now. Noah was

a joy. Galina was taking an extended leave from school to tend to Arvy, and Erik was in my home, most nights in my bed. My life was so sweet and bright, and that was showing in my game. The Railers had shaken off the slump and were now playing with fire again. My goals against average was going down while my saves were climbing.

I'd not felt this good in many years, and I wanted to make sure Erik knew how special he was to me. I'd taken time searching for the perfect Valentine's Day gift for him. Adler had many suggestions. Most involved gold and diamonds. Tennant told me to give him a gift from my heart, but I had no idea what that meant. After a game last week in Philly, I'd asked Trent for gift advice that I could find without making my brain hurt from thinking. He'd pulled me aside and showed me a little website that he liked to visit.

"Trust me, you give him this and a dozen roses and he'll be yours for the taking."

"I no say this for man," I hurried to clarify. Trent reached up to pat my cheek, and walked off, his hips swaying as he went to find Dieter. It was okay that he knew even if I didn't know how he knew. Trent would never out Erik and me, and I liked him. He had made me faster and his clothes were bright and festive.

The morning of Valentine's Day, I woke Erik with a soft kiss to his neck that led to soft kisses on his mouth, my fingers wound in his curls, until he was as hard as I was.

"Lay back. I have good gift for you."

His green eyes were warm as an enchanted fire I'd seen in a video game. Just as magical, too.

I left him in my bed for just a moment, grabbed the small bag from my underwear drawer, and returned to him. He moved to sit up. I put a hand on his chest and applied pressure, keeping his back to the thick mattress.

"My gift for you is reservations tonight at Le Button," he said while pawing in the gift bag. I folded my legs under me, using my calves as a seat. His eyes narrowed a bit when he removed the tub with the silver and red ribbons dangling from it. Spinning the container around, he saw the label and smiled a sinful smile.

"Chocolate body paint?"

"Yes. I paint you and lick it off. Make fun times."

"Thinking about doing this tonight is going to make me hot all day."

"We do now." I plucked the tub from his hands, spun the top off, and inhaled the scent of chocolate. Then I shook the soft paint brush from the gift bag. "Must make warm. Go nowhere."

Thundering down the stairs with my hard dick bouncing, I threw the jar into the microwave above the stove, and waited. As soon as it pinged, I flung the door on the microwave open, grabbed the warm jar, and raced back to my room. Galina's door was open, so I hurried by, using the jar to hide my genitals. I ran to my lover, eager to paint his body.

Stepping into the master suite, I nearly fell over my big feet when my gaze landed on Erik. He had stayed right where I had told him to. His fist worked his cock lazily. His tongue ran out to slick his lips. My cock throbbed harder.

"Hands and knees," I said, my voice thick with desire.

He followed that order quickly, his ass up in the air, his arms spread out in front of him as he rested his nose in the covers and pillows.

"I paint your ass then lick it clean. Then your balls. Then I cover your cock and let you slide it down my throat." I placed the warm chocolate on the nightstand, grabbed his hips, and tugged hard. When his knees were on the edge of the mattress, I took a moment to enjoy the sight of his puckered hole bared for me, of his heavy balls, and of his thick cock dangling low. I would taste all of them before the sun rose properly.

"Stan…" He was breathy and needy. I cupped a buttock, squeezed it firmly, then went for the chocolate. The brush was overloaded with sweetness. Thick drops hit the carpet and the cover. I made a wide swath of chocolate from the base of his spine down to his nuts. "Oh… that's nice."

"This nicer." I poured some over the crack of his ass and watched it run down over his hole. Then, with little regard to the jar or how it sat on the bed, I went to my knees and buried my face between his slippery ass-cheeks.

"Ah, hell yeah, so much nicer!"

He pressed back as my tongue teased his entrance. I licked and lapped, pressing into his tight hole, then kissing it, swirling my tongue around and in, around and in, around and in, sucking and groaning. Erik was done talking. Gibberish in fractured Swedish tangled with my gruff dirty words in Russian.

I moved from his ass to his balls, pulling one tender orb into my mouth, tugging on it, sucking it hard then moving to the right. I did that many times, my fingers dipping into the jar now to coat his ass again. His hips moved up and back with more speed. I feasted on his ass and balls, using almost the whole sixteen-ounce jar. Melted chocolate was everywhere, and it was a sticky-sweet delight that I wanted more of. Fingers thick with the last of the cooling treat, I coated his cock, then sat on the floor, letting my head rest on the mattress.

I led his cock to my mouth, and he took over from there. His thrusts were deep, primal, as he balanced on the edge of an orgasm. I took my cock in hand and tugged on it, fingers slick with chocolate. Erik fucked my mouth well and hard, coming with a shout. Spunk coated my mouth and throat. I pumped my dick faster, eager to join him. The delectable taste of Erik and milk chocolate got me off. I shot on my hand and thigh, sucking madly as Erik filled my mouth with short, quick thrusts.

"God, oh God, shit...holy hell," he panted, my tongue gliding over the smooth head of his cock as he gently slowed his pace.

"Mmm," I hummed around his cock. He groaned and trembled. "Sweetest treat ever," I whispered, taking the time to lick him clean.

"We need to get more of that stuff," he chuckled, then rolled onto his back, his beautiful cock popping free of my lips. I ran my fingers through the semen on my leg, my eyes closed, dreamily lost in the afterglow of passion.

"I thank Trent most big. He show me good interweb site. Many hot sex fun things."

"Trent rocks."

"I think my ass glued to blanket by chocolate," I said a moment later. Erik laughed softly above me, then crawled off the bed. I opened my eyes and found a Norse god standing over me, cock spent and soft, thighs coated with chocolate, and eyes dewy with love.

"Let me clean that ass for you." He offered me a hand.

We went into the shower, hands greedily roaming over each other. "I love you," I moaned into his ear as his soapy hands lathered my ass. "You make life complete, you and Noah—is like dream coming true."

He arched into me, his cock plumping up, his fingers sliding up from my ass to my back. "Living the dream, aren't we?" Erik rose to his toes to bite at my jaw.

I made love to him in the shower, burying myself in his hot, tight body, all the while telling him how I adored him, worshiped him, loved him madly. And, to my joy, he repeated all the love words back to me.

After our passionate shower, we dried off and shaved, talking low and familiar, like lovers or partners do. Planning the day, discussing the super fancy dinner out Erik had planned for us tonight. We dressed quickly, Erik grabbed the baby monitor, and we slipped into the hall.

We snuck past Galina's door, then checked on Noah. The baby was sleeping soundly, so we went to the kitchen and started cooking. I was ravenous, so Erik decided to make his special waffles with blueberries. Over the baby monitor, Noah started jabbering to his new blue teddy bear that shared his crib.

"You make waffle. I get Noah and wake Galina. She love your waffles much."

"Kiss me first."

I did, with fire, then I jogged back up the stairs to get Noah. He was smiling but wet. After a complete change of clothes and a dry diaper, I picked him up and cuddled him. Such a good, happy baby. I kissed his soft cheek, glad I had shaved the thick, dark, rough whiskers from my face.

"Come, we go wake Galina. Watch her eat many waffles."

"Bah!" He patted my face as we made our way to the room my sister occupied. Shuffling the heavy boy to my hip, I knocked on the doorframe.

"Wake up for waffle time," I called around the cracked door.

"Bah, bah, bah, GAH!" Noah shouted. I peeked around the door to see her bed neatly made, a small note propped against one of several rose-colored throw pillows.

Slipping into the feminine room, I walked to the bed and lifted the note from the thick duvet.

"She spend much time with Arvy," I explained to Noah in case he was looking for Galina. Shaking the paper open, I bounced Noah on my hip as I read the neatly penned note to Noah. It was in Russian, but I read it in English for him. Someday I hoped to teach him Russian. Erik will teach him Swedish. He will be the smartest boy in his preschool.

"Dear Stan," I smiled at my...Erik's boy chewing on a fist. "Do not be mad."

Oh. That's not a good way to start a letter.

"What has she done now? If she is making to drop off school to make whoopy with Arvy, I will be most mad," I told Noah.

"Bah."

"Yes, that would be most bad." My gaze went back to the letter. "I am not in trouble. I am in Las Vegas."

I lifted my gaze from the note. Las Vegas? Why is she there? To see our next game? But that was not until late tomorrow.

"Maybe they wish to gamble and see shows," I told Noah. "Viva Las Vegas."

"Bah."

"Yes, much Elvis. I will seek blue suede baby shoes for you when there over weekend."

Noah began to wiggle. I read faster.

"She is with Arvy. They are so happy in love and she knows this is for the right, so she does not want me to be mad about them getting married."

"Bah?"

I stared at the letter for so long my eyes got dry. Erik shouted up the stairs that the waffles were ready, and Galina had better hurry or he would eat them all. I stalked out of her room, the letter in my hand, and went down the stairs like an angry elephant.

Erik looked at me over his shoulder when I stormed into the kitchen, his soft smile fading when he saw my face.

"What's wrong?" He turned from the waffle maker with a plate piled high with blueberry waffles.

"Galina has troped with Arvy!" I growled, and shook the paper in his face. He blinked at me. "She has run off to marry him! Using ladder and sneaking off from window. Troped! Troped!"

"Eloped," he said as he took his son from me.

I filled the kitchen with Russian expletives as I balled the note and whipped it into the trash. "Call nanny. We go to Las Vegas now. I kill him for sneaking off with my sister! She has big wedding plans in church. Mama will shit cow when she hears!"

"Stan, take a breath." He buckled the baby into his high chair. I took several. It didn't help. "Did she say why they'd run off? I didn't think people did that anymore."

"She no say, but she will—you make trusts me she will tell me!"

Erik tried to tell me things while I made reservations for the first flight to Las Vegas. Things like I needed to calm down, we had a game there tomorrow so why not wait to find her then, and to calm down. He said to calm down the most. He was still telling me to calm down when we landed at the McCarran International Airport four hours later. He should know by now that Russians do not calm down. We find the problem and beat it into no longer being a problem. Arvy would no longer be a problem.

In the back of a cab that smelled like purple onions, I called my sister. Again. For the fortieth time. "If she does no answer my head will make explosion," I told Erik.

"Coach was not happy about us taking off and missing morning skate," he sighed as desert rolled past. I grumbled in Russian as Galina's phone rang and rang. "She's not going to answer."

No, she wouldn't, but to my surprise, Arvy did. "Stan," he started, "let me explain."

"Where are you with my sister?"

"Stan, we have a good reason."

"I have good reason to make boot go up your fucking ass."

"Okay, yeah, maybe…"

"Where are you with my sister?" I repeated, Galina now bitching at Arvy for answering her phone while she was in the bathroom.

"A tiny chapel on the strip. It's white and pink and has a big statue of Elvis out front."

"We be there ten minutes. Marry her before I get there I will have you killed. I know people. They will make your eyeballs disappear and leave your body in the desert for the coo-hoots to eat."

"Coyotes," Erik yelled for clarification. I hung up on Arvy and my now-angry sister. The bright-light city did not set my soul on fire. Slamming into the small chapel and seeing my sister and stupid Arvy who was on crutches did that. I lunged at my fellow Railer. Erik leaped between us, using all his strength to push me in reverse so my hands didn't go around Arvy's neck.

"Stanislav!" Galina slapped at my arms, her blows making more pain than I'd ever admit. "Stop it! Hitting a man on crutches is low! You have no say, *no say*, in who I marry!"

Erik wrapped his arms around me, pushing steadily back as I tried to move forward.

"I have all say! I am man of family. You know Mama want church wedding for you. Only child who can marry in our church. You know this! Why break Mama heart?!"

Arvy dropped down to sit in a pew, his crutches making noise as they fell off the wooden seat to the floor. Galina stopped hitting me. Erik didn't let go of me.

"I had no choice. I love him," she said, her big gray eyes still lit with Soviet fire. "I know Russia and America are not on good terms. They do away with exchange students, my visa is only temporary. I want to live here with him, go to school here, work here and make a family like you and Erik have done."

"You can do this without marriage. You know him two months!"

"I know I love him and this is best way for me to stay in America." She tipped her chin up and folded her arms over her breast. I did the same. Well, I jerked my chin up. Crossing my arms was impossible, since Erik was still glued to my chest. A skinny man with a big black wig peeked through some white-and-gold curtains.

"That is the preacher. We're next. Will you be a good brother and give me to Arvy?"

I stared daggers at the man in the sequined jumpsuit. Erik slowly released his hold on me and stepped back, just an inch in case I tried to get to Arvy again.

"Arvy, do you love my sister tender and true?"

He stood up and stood behind her. "Yes, I do."

I looked deep into his eyes and saw truth. "If you hurt her or look puck bunnies on the road, I have you killed. I know people." I pointed at his left eye.

"Right, yeah, I got that. Eyeballs and coyotes. I will never hurt her. Ever. You have my word." He extended his hand to me.

"Arvy is a good man, Stan, you know that," Erik whispered to me, his firm body at my side calming.

I wasn't finished. "When season is over, we have big wedding. In church for Mama. I pay. You say no, I make call to eyeball pluckers," I said to Arvy. Galina rolled her eyes.

"That's fine. I want to marry her right and keep my eyeballs."

I took his hand and pumped it. Once. Just once. My sister stepped up to me, her eyes less angry. I pulled her to me and hugged her hard.

"You are my sweet little bird," I cooed as I ran my hand over her long, dark hair. "If he does one thing wrong…"

"I will call the eyeball pluckers myself." She went to her tippy-toes to kiss my cheek. "Come, walk me down the aisle."

I glanced at Erik. He smiled and nodded, and went to sit in the front pew.

All too soon it was done—my sister had been given to Arvid Ulfsson and was now repeating vows fed to her by the Elvis impersonator. Erik sat beside me, his arm and leg pressed to mine. I could smell his shampoo. His leg was warm and strong. I leaned to the left just a bit.

"Thank you for stop me kill him," I whispered.

He smiled gently and let his curls rest on my shoulder. I took his hand and threaded my fingers through his.

"All part of loving a wild Bolshevik," he replied in soft tones.

"Good thing I have Swedish in life to be calm neutral."

"*Very* good thing, or we'd have a Railer with no eyeballs and coyote bite marks all over his face," he chuckled as Elvis blessed the couple, then threw sequins at them instead of rice. Ah, America. What a wonderful country.

FIFTEEN

Erik

S tan was quiet on the way to the arena. Didn't matter
that we'd just come from a wedding, we had to switch
to hockey mode, and we'd already fucked up by missing
optional skate. A family emergency for one of us? Coach
could handle that. But both of us?

Which was why me and my quiet lover were now in the
small visiting team office, standing in front of Coach
Benning and waiting for the shit to hit the fan.

I wondered if we should get our player rep up here.
Toly was the kind of person you needed in the room when
you were going to be hauled over the coals. Or maybe we
should get Connor in; maybe our captain would be a
calming influence.

Coach Benning regarded us steadily.

"I don't want to know," he began. "Stan?"

Stan looked confused, and I didn't blame him. Was the
simple use of Stan's name with a question mark on the end
of it a request for an explanation, even though Benning
said he didn't want to know?

"I don't think Stan knows what you mean."

Stan shot me a look and scowled. "I'm talk self," he said, and I left him to it. He'd been so happy after he'd accepted the whole Arvy-marrying-his-sister thing, and then something had changed.

"And?" Benning prompted. "Do I put you in net tonight? Is your head straight?"

Stan blinked at him and rolled his neck. "Head is fine."

"I mean, are you okay?" Benning asked in plainer English.

"Vegas pipes need me," Stan said, then he nodded and left the room. Walked out on Coach, and I knew damn well that he'd get away with that shit because of his weird goalie reputation.

Me, on the other hand, I was fourth line.

"He needed you to go with him?" Benning asked, indicating the closed door that Stan had just shut. That was a loaded question. If I hadn't, then Arvy would have been "vanished" into the desert never to be seen again.

"Yes, Coach," I answered, simple and truthful.

He seemed way too thoughtful, and I imagined my start tonight was in danger of becoming a healthy scratch.

"See the PT before the game. You're favoring your left leg."

"Okay, Coach."

I turned to leave, assuming I was in the game, that I hadn't been scratched, but until I managed to get out of the room, who knew what the hell would happen? I got as far as having my hand on the doorknob.

"And Gunner?" My heart fell, and I slowly turned to face him.

"Yes, Coach?"

"I'm fining you and Stan ten thousand each. Also, you will never miss a team flight again. Fair?"

I nodded, because yeah, that was fair. "Yes, Coach, thank you."

Coach Benning shook his head. "Don't thank me—thank Toly and Connor, who separately felt they needed to come to your rescue like you were two damsels in fucking distress rather than grown fucking men. And for fuck's sake, score a fucking goal tonight."

I left before he got more wound up. In fact, Coach wasn't one of those guys who cursed a lot, and I think every other word in his last sentence was "fuck".

Toly was outside the room, Charlie next to him, and I felt a swell of gratitude that my line was there to back me up.

"Arvy texted me," Toly announced.

"And me," Charlie added.

Seemed like Arvy had called in support from Stan's fellow Russian for him, and Charlie, who was possibly the closest I had to a friend on the team, for me.

Toly left, I fist-bumped Charlie, and together we headed for the locker room. There was no official skate that morning, not on game day, but we all worked on conditioning, and yeah, I was favoring my left leg after a particularly shitty check had me hitting the boards at an angle.

The sports PT tutted at the range of motion in my leg, announced it wasn't optimal, then pummeled the offending set of muscles and ligaments into submission. An ice bath later, and I was ready to say I was retiring to get away from the torture.

Until I pulled on skates and uniform and followed Toly onto the ice for warmups. Then I remembered exactly why I went through the pain. Hockey.

Stan was there, crouching in front of his pipes, staring out at center ice, his body rigid, his focus absolute. I wanted to go over and stick-tap his blocker, but didn't, instead skating lazy circles around the net and coming back to the blue line. The stands weren't full—this was warmups —but there was a strong contingent of Railers fans who were at the glass with signs. Mostly for Ten, who despite coming out as gay and in a relationship, was still fawned over by the entire female fan base, and to be fair quite a lot of the males as well. I think it helped that Ten was the star of our team; maybe him being gay was more acceptable all the time he was scoring and dragging us closer to the play-offs. Hell, he was tied for second place in the entire freaking league for points.

One sign caught my eye, a huge picture of Ten and a bright flash of white over his head on black card. I read the words, *God Hates Fags*, and felt sick, sliding to a stop right in front of it and staring at the guy holding it. I was blocking everyone's view, and fuck knows how I was going to stop Ten from seeing it. Someone skated up next to me. Ten. I didn't even have to look to see who it was, he just had this way about him—a confidence and speed, and his voice was firm.

"I already saw it," he murmured.

"How did he even get that fucking thing in here?"

"Coach is calling security," Ten said.

My heart ached for the kid. Why was it so wrong to be in love? Why did people have to judge you for it?

Someone else joined us.

"Wassup?" Toly asked, echoed by Charlie, who also joined us. Soon the entire Railers team stood nose to nose with the asshole, who was fucking brave with the glass between us. He faltered a little, the sign drooped, and then somehow, he must have found resolve, because he spat at the glass. The people next to him, the ones with signs that loved on the team and Ten, stepped away, looking at the man in horror. He was nothing special, not much more than a kid himself, wild-eyed, his long hair hanging around his face.

He smiled, then, his grin obscene as security arrived and politely asked him to get the hell out. I would have punched him to the ground, but Ten, he just shook his head and skated backward and away. The guy with the sign struggled and ended up on the floor, his sign thrown down and left as he was escorted away. A small girl, no more than ten or so, picked up the sign. She frowned, then took out a Sharpie and crossed out the evil words, turning the sign so we could see what it said now. *We love the Railers,* with a big heart in the white space.

I blew her a kiss, and smiled, and she dipped her head in embarrassment. I tossed her a puck, and she grinned at me. That was the kind of fan we wanted, the one who just loved hockey and knew that if a player was good, then they should play. Simple.

I don't know if it was that gesture of team solidarity, but we played our hearts out. Stan with a shutout, me with my tenth goal of the season, and Max with a Gordie Howe hat trick—a goal, an assist and a fight—and now missing a tooth after taking a puck to the jaw with seconds left in the third. I collected the puck for Stan so he could keep it to celebrate his shut-out. The entire team stick-tapped him as we did the whole head-bump thing post-game. That was us saying thank you to the man in the pipes.

Our man.

No. *Mine.*

"Am needing little bit talk," Stan announced after we got back to the hotel. He wasn't quiet anymore; he'd laughed and joked with the team after the game, still on a high from the shut-out. There had been forty-one shots on goal, and insanely, he and the defense had stopped every single one.

But he'd been quiet in the coach to the hotel, his head-phones in, and I'd kind of wanted to pull out his earbuds and ask what the hell was going on. I hadn't, because I'd guessed he needed space.

"Okay," I said, uncertainly. We normally made every show of going to our separate rooms, but this time Stan took my hand and pulled me from the empty elevator straight to his room. I attempted to tug free—this was way too dangerous—but he gripped tight, and when we were finally in his room, he pulled me so close I could hardly breathe.

"I'm love you little bit lot," he announced.

"Okay, I love you too," I replied, muffled against his neck.

"Marry me," he blurted out. "One day, in future. Time later."

"Yes," I said, without hesitation, because one day, maybe after our careers were done, when his mom was safe here, when it was okay to be out and not have hate, when I could be as brave as Ten, then we could get married.

Stan simply held me tighter.

TWO WEEKS PASSED before what I like to call the Freja event. Finally, we had all the paperwork with the right codes and lines and whatever. I thought it was as simple as me signing and sending back, but no, Freja was in the country and the text I received said *'wouldn't it be so cool to meet up and sign. I could meet Noah'*.

Cool wasn't the first thing that came to mind, and I

was torn. Her text said she'd like to see Noah, and that was okay. Wasn't it?

"What if she loves him?" That was my biggest fear, and after the third time of saying it in various ways, looking for a reaction from Stan, he finally said something back.

He picked Noah up and kissed his cheeks. His face was covered with soft stubble, the beginnings of what he liked to call his pre-playoff beard. He smiled at me. "Of course, all peoples loves little rabbit."

He didn't seem to see a problem in that statement, and I desperately wanted to shake him to get him to see that I was worried. Freja hadn't wanted to be pregnant, or have a child, but there was a big difference between handing over a tiny, squalling baby and seeing this gorgeous child who was nearly walking and had even managed a *Dah* with his *bah*s. He would be one soon, his birthday only a few weeks away, and I couldn't bring myself to imagine a life where I didn't have Noah with me.

"You don't understand," I snapped, reaching for Noah, and Stan let me have him. I needed to cuddle my son and escape big Russians who had no idea what I was feeling. I'd made it to the kitchen door in my attempt to escape when it hit me that I was expecting Stan to comprehend my worries when I hadn't even told him.

I stopped and turned, holding Noah close.

"What if she sees him, and loves him so much that she wants equal custody, and I lose him. Who the hell in their right minds would trust a hockey player with a baby, and…" I subsided into silence, because any words I let spill out would damage us as a unit, I could see that clearly.

I expected Stan to reassure me, blindly tell me that everything would be okay.

"I'm think same," he admitted, and sat heavily on the nearest stool.

When he said that, I knew that was what I'd needed him to say; that he shared my fear. I went back to him immediately. I had an hour before the meeting, Noah needed changing and dressing, and I was still in sweats after my shower. Stan hugged us both, and we stood there for a long time, drawing strength from each other. We'd decided last night that Stan wouldn't go with me, even though he wanted to, and god, I wanted him to be with me.

We had to be sensible.

FACED WITH FREJA, with all her icy beauty and the way she commanded the room, it was another thing altogether. I hadn't remembered her as being quite so together, but then we'd had sex twice, and the next time we'd met she'd been a mess, three months pregnant and not knowing what to do.

We signed the divorce forms. It was a formality and easily done, despite Noah bouncing on my leg and gripping my hair, with an added *bah* every so often.

The lawyers pulled out the next sheaf of papers. This was the big one, the final signing for Freja relinquishing any claim on Noah. I hadn't wanted that to start with, had told her she should have a solid presence in her son's life. She hadn't wanted it then, but what if she wanted it now?

"He looks well," she commented, and I saw the soft smile on her face, "and a lot like you."

What did I say to that? Did I brag that my son was the greatest child in the entire universe of children, or dismiss what she was saying so that it didn't give her ideas of wanting him?

I'm a mess. I'm losing my mind.

"Thank you," I responded.

"Dah bah," Noah added.

She looked at me, thoughtful, then pulled the papers toward her and signed them. In a flurry of leather and silk, she stood up and pressed a kiss to Noah's head and then to mine.

"I read an article," she began, and took the chair next to mine, holding my hand. "Well, many of them, actually, about how a woman can walk away from a baby, what is inside her that makes her cold to what she nurtured for nine months."

"Freja—"

"No, let me finish. I will always have a place in my heart for Noah, that is a biological imperative. I don't see him as mine, but you can tell him I will never regret having him. But, also that I knew I would never be half the parent that you can be to him. You have to promise me you will tell him that always."

"I will, but Freja, you can still visit and tell him this yourself?"

She shook her head. "No, not for a while. When he's older, maybe, and I can explain that I wasn't right for him. There's something else, though." The lawyers shuffled paper and were talking to each other soft and low, and she turned to them. "Can we have the room a moment, please?"

They left, although my lawyer looked pissed, probably thinking she would be talking me around to giving her Noah.

"What is it?" I asked, cautious and worried at the same time.

She handed me an envelope. "There's a check in there, for every penny I said I needed from you to keep Noah to term."

"What? Freja, that's yours——"

"I didn't want it then, and I still don't. I was angry. I wanted to make you pay because you forced me to listen to my heart. I can't adequately explain, but I want you to know, I do love the idea of Noah in my own way. I don't want him to know that I tried to drive you away with demanding money."

"Is that what you were doing?"

"I think so. But, I never want him to think that you had to buy him. Because that wasn't true, there isn't a price on a child. He is with his father, and that is where he should be."

My heart felt lighter, but I couldn't stop the tears that pricked my eyes. She kissed me then, on the end of my nose, and did the same again to Noah.

"Sign the papers, Erik," she whispered, and pushed them toward me. "You don't owe me a thing, but please, don't let Noah hate me."

I signed where the post-it note indicated, and it was done. She was wrong, I owed her everything. She'd given me Noah.

She smiled and moved to leave, but I grabbed her hand and held her, made her turn back to me.

"He will always know you wanted the best for him," I promised.

And I meant every word.

THINGS SETTLED SO QUICKLY into normality.

It was *normal* that Stan made a final move to my room, right next to Noah, and that it became our room. Freja's words stayed with me, and it became normal that I made sure to tell Noah every day that his mom loved him and that she wanted the best for him.

Normal was nice, and the hockey that came with the solid, stable family I was creating was some of the best of my life.

Tomorrow we played Dallas, and winning two points meant we were on our way to being safe into the playoffs. The Stanley Cup was right within our reach. The buzz in the room was that of a team of winners.

Skate today was practicing line rushes, and Stan chirped everyone whether they got a goal past him or not. Of course, Ten was first to score—did this fancy deke that had Stan landing like a turtle on his back, laughing like a loon, and then cursing Ten out in loud Russian. Ten punched the air and skated back with his line, grinning widely, chirping at Stan for not getting up.

I loved this team, standing with Toly and Charlie, waiting for our line to go against Stan. I watched his every move, judged if he was going easy, was he leaving his five-hole open, was he slow with the blocker, was there any single minute thing he was doing wrong that I could use?

Then it hit me. I was always looking for the angle, the break in his concentration, the mistake, and trying to be clever. I didn't need to be. We set off, from Toly to me, to Charlie, and then to me, and straight on, without hesitation, I let a slap-shot go that clipped the posts and ricocheted into the net, passing Stan, who had been expecting me to go left or right.

I fist-pumped, and he grinned at me, and all I wanted to do was go up and kiss the grin right off his face.

I didn't.

Instead, I chirped him about being a sieve, and got a load of abuse back about my parentage.

God, I loved hockey.

SIXTEEN

Stan

"Noah, is good yams. See? Mm-Mm good." I took a spoonful of the mashed yams and gagged. "Okay, is not good. I make eggs."

"Bah." He slapped his tray with his spoon.

"Yes, eggs good for big boy."

I pushed back from the kitchen table and went to the fridge to take out the eggs. The house was quiet this morning, but that was because it was only five o'clock and Erik was sleeping off a game-winning goal followed by a good fuck last night. He was in my bed. I found great joy in waking up with him beside me, or sprawled over me, his curls flattened from sleep or badly knotted from sex. We were in the same room now; I'd long given up the pretense of going back to my own room. I looked out at the starry sky. Worry nibbled at my heart. So much could go wrong…

"Bah. Dah. Blibbity."

"Ah yes, I think music good too."

I smiled as I cracked egg after egg into a large frying pan. The boy talked nonstop but said nothing anyone could understand. Adler said that was me rubbing off on him. As the eggs began to cook, I reached over to turn on the fancy Bose radio on the counter. Elvis filled the kitchen just as the sun began to peek through the trees. Daylight was earlier and earlier now that April was here. It was good to be rid of the cold of winter. Maybe we could clean up the yard and get some fencing put up. Maybe a dog! Yes. Oh, a dog. Big one, like a wolfhound that would rip the face off anyone who tried to climb over the fence to touch my son. Erik's son, I mean.

"Eggs is soon," I told the boy, then sat down in front of him and picked up a stuffed teddy bear from the floor by a sodden ear. "Why eat bear ear?" I asked the lad. He made grabby hands for the teddy. Elvis started singing a song about wanting to be someone's teddy bear, so I made the blue bear with the wet ear dance for Noah. He squealed in joy. I continued with the dancing and then sang along.

"I didn't know breakfast came with a floor show," Erik called from the doorway, smiling widely while looking beyond beautiful in low-riding sleep pants, his new tattoo on his bicep, and little else. He'd gone yesterday to have Noah's name on his skin, but then he'd added my name, all twisted with a tiny blue-and-gray Pokémon character—Cranados, or so Ten reminded me. He said it reminded him of me, a rock, immoveable in my net. His belly had tiny suck marks on it. I loved seeing my love bites on his pale skin. It made my balls heavy with want. He was so handsome, so hot, and now, finally, so mine.

"Show is only for Noah," I replied as he went over to kiss his son on the head then grab a taste of my mouth.

"Ugh. You taste like unsweetened yams." Erik made a face that got a giggle from Noah.

"Most sorry. I get coffee. You kiss again."

That was what happened. A hot coffee kiss until the

eggs in the pan were past needing attention. Erik scraped the mess out and started over, tending to the food while I sipped coffee and made Blue Bear dance.

"What got you up so early?" Erik asked, placing a plate filled with fluffy eggs and dark wheat toast in front of me. Noah got loud until his eggs were served. The spoon went flying and he used his hands.

"What if they keep Galina because not like to marry Arvy? What if they won't let Mama leave? What if they know we are gay men and put in prison?"

"Stan, everything will be fine. They both have all the proper papers. The Railers lawyers went over visas and student papers for Galina to study here with fine tooth combs."

"Yes, yes, I know. Fine combs, but still…"

"They'll be fine."

"Oh, yes, I know. Is all good. Still…" I glanced at the wide windows looking out at our backyard. The sky was still dark, but soon it would be bright pink and purple. And somewhere under that sky, on the other side of the world, were my sister and mother, hopefully getting into a plane to come to America.

"Stan, your mother is coming. There is no way she's not going to be here to get to know Noah."

"Yes, yes, I know. She wants to be *babushka* to him much bad."

"Yep." He nodded, sending several golden curls on his brow bouncing. "I think it's amazing how all it took to lure her here was knowing there was a baby in our house. Your house."

"No, no fix. Is our house." I reached over to lay my hand over his. His gaze touched our hands, then came back to me. "Will always be our house. When Mama here, free from Russia and bad gay hate there, we make home

163

right. No more lie about us. Say we live here as couple. Just…not big out-coming. Quiet. Just be. Yes?"

"Yes." He slipped his fingers between mine. His eyes glowed like fiery emeralds.

"BAH!" Scrambled eggs slapped Erik in the face. I snorted. His green eyes went wide. Then a sweet smile pulled up the corners of his coffee-kissed lips. Soon my family would be complete. By midnight, life would be all I had dreamed it would be.

But just to make sure, I would stop by the Russian Orthodox church on the way to the arena for morning skate, and pray. I didn't think God would ignore my pleas because I shared coffee kisses with a man.

AMY WAS WITH NOAH, and Erik had driven us to the rink. I checked my watch. Why had Galina not contacted me at the airport as I had asked? Had there been trouble?

"Stan. Give me that watch."

I looked over at Erik after we pulled into a parking spot by the players' entrance. "No. I need for time looks."

"Looking at it every five seconds is just going to make the time drag." He turned off the engine of the car we shared. I had bought it for him but told him that I had purchased it for me. See how clever I am? He would never drive it if it was a gift for him. His pride was huge. Which was good, but not always. I reminded him often about pride going before a fall.

I tugged down the sleeve of my dress shirt and soft gray suit jacket. "I keep but no look."

He ran a hand over my head, his touch tender and loving. "It'll be fine. Have faith. You prayed, right?"

"Yes, right. God knows. Is in his hands now." I nodded.

We left the Caddy—a big blue SUV, not a pink one—and went inside. Pete stopped us, and we talked about the few remaining games of the season. The playoffs were on the horizon, and the Railers were tied with Pittsburgh for first place. Philadelphia was one point behind the two leaders. And the team under them only lacked a point from being in second. Our division was tighter than a homecoming dress, as Adler says.

The dressing room was packed with men, all talking and in good spirits. It made me feel brighter inside. Not totally sunny but maybe partly cloudy.

"Hey, it's Van Helsing!" Adler shouted, then threw a big grin at Max van Hellren entering the room. Max was a solid defenseman who had played on almost every team during his tenure in the league. He was a huge man, with reddish-brown hair and a thick beard that he kept neatly trimmed.

His golden-brown eyes were sharp as a raptor's, but usually friendly, unless you were trying to make a run at me. Then the "Wrath of Hell" fell on opposing players. Max had made a big splash on the team, filling in for Arvy, who was now about ready to start skating with a no-contact jersey during practice. I hoped Max stayed. He brought grit and gruff humor.

"I'm going to slap the stupid out of you, Lockhart," Max shouted over the guffaws.

"You'll have to catch me first, Gramps," Adler yelled back.

This was how it had been since the first day Max had entered the Railers dressing room. Adler had yelled, "Hey, it's Van Halen!" at Max back then, and Max had threatened to slap him shitless, or silly, or into the next week. It was tradition now.

Erik and I exchanged soft looks as we dressed. Like

Tennant and Jared, we played down our relationship at work. Even more so because no one knew we were a couple aside from a few close friends. We had no plans to make a big thing out of us. We just wanted to be.

After gearing up, I went to the ice to work with my coach. Stepping into the corridor, I bumped into a beautiful black man with a dog on a leash.

"Am sorry," I said to him, then crouched down to pet the dog. It was a tiny one with kinky black fur. It wagged its tail and licked my face. "Such good dog! Why is dog here?"

"I'm Ben, the manager of the Crossroads Shelter over on Grayson Street. The team invited us to come out during the first and second periods and bring a shelter animal in need of a home."

"This boy needs home? I need big dog. Like wolfhound. Will this dog be wolfhound?"

"Nope, that's as big as he gets," Ben replied with a killer smile.

"Cute," Max said around his mouth guard as he came up beside me. I glanced up from the dog. Was our grinder talking about the dog or Ben? It was hard to tell. Both men were staring at each other. Then Max was gone, heading to the ice.

"We look for dog soon. Come to shelter. Make yard fence first."

Ben nodded dully, mumbled something, handed me a business card, then disappeared into the bowels of the arena, his happy dog trotting along beside him.

"So we're getting a dog now?" Erik asked as he jogged up behind me, his skates making a dull thudding sound as the guards hit the rubber mat.

"Yes, big dog. Eat face off people who come into yard. Keep Noah safe." I nodded as if that was the end of the discussion. The Czar had spoken.

"Yeah, we'll talk about the big face-eating dog," he said, then hustled ahead of me. So much for the Czar having last say. My house was a democracy now. Fitting as this *was* America.

I found Coach Madsen on the ice and skated to him, my cell phone in my catcher.

"If sister call or text, come tell me. Much please and thank you."

Coach Madsen plucked the phone from my big mitt and slid it into the inner pocket of his suit coat.

"I'll make a beeline for you if this so much as twitches." He patted his breast.

"Is good friend make beeline." I cuffed him on the shoulder. "What is beeline?"

He rolled his arm a bit after I tapped him. "It means I'll come straight to you. Like a bee flies."

"But bee no fly straight. Bee go from flower to flower, sucking sweet, in funky curl lines." I drew circles in the air with my finger.

Coach Madsen made that face. It was the face people make at me often when I point out that English sayings are not sensible sometimes.

"Okay, right, that's true."

"So, why is saying beeline if go straight? Why not say cowline? Cow go straight."

"I don't know why it's not a cowline, Stan, it's a beeline."

"Also bird fly straight. As crow flies. Maybe say birdline." I nodded. Coach stared up at me. I waited for him to say something.

"Fine, I'll make a birdline to you if this so much as twitches."

"Ah, good. Making sense. Thanks. I make saves now."

"You do that."

I skated to my pipes. Then I touched them. Stroked them. Whispered to them in sweet mother tongue. They hummed back, icy cold to the touch but warm to my ears.

"*Moya lyubov k tebe gluboka I verna.*" "My love for you is deep and true," I told them as the team made laps around the ice to get the blood flowing.

"Didn't you say that to me last night?" Erik said, coming to a short stop and spraying me with ice.

"Yes. What is point?"

"You're cheating on your pipes with me," he teased, gave me a saucy wink, then skated off to catch Tennant, which no one could but they all tried.

I chuckled. What a silly man. Still, I talked extra-long to my pipes that morning in case they got jealous.

MY PIPES KNEW I was true to them and they treated me well. Through scrimmages where no one scored to an important game with Florida where also no one scored. The middle Rowe brother, Jamie, tried, but I was tight in the head. That was what Ten had said. Tight in the head.

After the game, the team and Jamie were meeting somewhere to eat and drink beer. Erik and I were not going. He was taking me to the airport to pick up my sister and my mother. Usually after a game, I'm ravenous, but tonight I was unable to eat or even think of food.

One quick text from Galina several hours ago. Ten hours to be exact. They had gotten onto the plane with no issues. Mama had even stopped to talk hockey with one of the men who checks baggage. That was why I had shut out Florida and Jamie Rowe. My breast was filled with so much happiness.

"You're smiling like Santa is about to land on your

rooftop," Erik commented as we waited inside the terminal. It was a busy airport in Harrisburg, with many gates. Not as big as others I had been in, but still a hustling place.

"Knowing Mama is safe is making me Santa happy."

Erik rubbed a hand over my back as I bounced up and down trying to see. Not that I had to do so. I easily saw over all the heads moving past, but I couldn't stop myself. I spotted Galina. Her dark head and beautiful gray eyes. She waved madly. I waved back and began muscling my way through the travelers coming and going. I had to move a fat man aside to see my mother.

She looked overwhelmed and scared. A thin, petite woman in a worn red coat, she stood out among the Americans dressed in the latest fashions. Galina pointed at me. Mama's loving gray eyes landed on me. She started crying. I gathered her to me and wept like Noah, long and hard, clinging to my mother. I murmured to her in Russian. She called me her baby boy over and over as she peppered my face with kisses. I reached for Galina and tugged her to my side. Mama under my left arm, Galina on my right.

Looking over my family, I saw Erik standing alone, smiling, dragging his hand under his eye.

I pulled away from my mother and sister, took Mama by the hand—such a tiny hand and so cold with uncertainty—and led her to Erik.

I slipped an arm around his waist. The first time I had ever engaged in such a public display of affection. To some it was nothing, but to us…it was everything.

"Mama, this is Erik. The man I love." I said that. In the airport. Tears threatened again.

She took his face in her work-rough hands and kissed his brow. "Noah," she said. The only word she knew in English, and it was his son's name. Mama prattled off a long line of questions, all in Russian. Erik looked at me.

"I will teach her good English. Like mine only gooder."

The ride home was filled with talking. Mostly Galina and Mama, but also me. I tried to keep Erik in the chatter, but the two women were discussing Arvy now. Mama was not happy that Galina had married outside of church. Galina was not happy that Mama was being old fashioned. Things were getting heated in the back until we pulled up to my house.

"Stanislav," Mama whispered in Russian, "this house is too fine for me."

"Never, Mama, never." I rushed to open her door and take her hand. Amy was awake, sitting with Noah, who was sound asleep in his crib upstairs. I took Mama through every room of my house, making the nursery last. Erik followed. Galina was tiffy, and went to see Arvy because she knew it would make Mama sputter.

"This house is so big. I'll need a map to find the kitchen," Mama said with good humor as we snuck into the nursery. Her kidding stopped when Erik scooped up his son and placed him in her waiting arms.

"*Vash vnuk*," he said, his Russian accent terrible but the words "your grandson" beautiful. We had practiced for weeks those two words, Erik insisting he be able to tell her that he considered her his son's other grandmother.

Mama's eyes grew wet with tears. She padded over to the heavy oak rocker by the window, sat down, and with Noah's curls resting on her shoulder, began to sing "*Bayu Bayushki Bayu*", the same song she had sung to my sister and me, and the one that I sang to Noah when I put him down for bed.

"I'm still not sure about songs where wolves come and drag little kids into the forest because they slept too close to the edge of the bed," Erik whispered, leaning in to me as we watched Mama and Noah rocking.

"Life is hard in Russia. Child is teached early."

"Hmmm."

I pressed a kiss to his curls. "I am happiest man ever."

"Life is good?"

Mama smiled up at us.

"Life is wonderful good. Is good for you?"

"It's wonderful good."

Epilogue

ERIK

Noah was spoiled for his first birthday. Seemed to me that everywhere I turned, someone was handing me gifts for him. Tiny Railers outfits from the equipment guys, the smallest hockey stick and puck I'd ever seen from Arvy and Galina, a savings bond from Connor, who said that every child should have a nest egg, and it didn't end there.

Stan and I bought up the entirety of a toy store, then hid a lot of it away when we got it home, because a one-year-old didn't really need a racing car game just yet, nor a set of metal construction pieces to build with.

Galina added extra bunnies to the mural so that it spread onto another wall, another family, all dressed in Railers uniforms. It was easy to identify Ten, and Arvy, and Stan in net, and me. She said she'd add in the Stanley Cup when we won it.

I pretended I hadn't heard her, because the superstitious part of me thought maybe mentioning it meant we wouldn't win. We weren't the favorites going in, drawn against Philadelphia in the first round. That didn't matter, though—we were a determined team.

The only dark spot on the horizon was the interview that needed to happen with Immigration for Galina and Arvy. They had to prove they'd married for love, but to be honest, anyone who saw them together knew they were in love. Or maybe I saw that because of how much I loved Stan. Who knows.

Stan was with Galina, thought that maybe his presence, NHL goalie brother with money, might add some support to her and Arvy's case. Which left me pacing the house, bouncing a fractious Noah, who was sucking on his fist through teething. I knew every corner of this huge place now, but still there was nowhere to hide from the worry.

Nor from Stan's momma, who didn't speak English, and was currently stalking me as I paced. She said something to me as I turned into the kitchen on my fifth walk-through.

She moved between me and the door I was about to go through, holding out her arms for Noah, and I passed him to her. She bobbled him, jiggled him, then handed him the cold gel teether that Stan had bought yesterday. The magic happened nearly instantly, Noah chewing and relaxing a little with each passing moment until finally he was quiet in her arms.

"Little rabbit," she said affectionately, in English, then smiled at me and patted my head.

This family thing? It really rocked.

Stan

"I SEE THIS IN MOVIE," I told a large woman sitting behind a desk. My sister and brother-in-law were having their green card interviews. In separate rooms. I was sitting out here with a woman who looked like she was trying to digest a porcupine. "Funny movie. Woman from Canada. Be sent back. Marries assistant. He is most pretty."

"*She* is most pretty, you mean," Grumpy Big Woman replied with no emotion.

"No, I mean he."

"Oh." She looked even more like a pokey animal was sitting in her bowels now.

"They go to place in Alaska. Make many funny things. Bird steal puppy. But drop, so puppy is fine. I get dog soon. Find good shelter run by handsome man. Big dog. Make loud woofs and eat men in brown shorts."

"And you're here in America for what reason?" She pursed her lips. Her lipstick was orange. Not a good color for her.

"I play hockey. Goalie. You know of hockey?" Her phone rang, but she ignored it to stare at me. I glanced behind me to see if something unsettling was there, but there was just a wall.

"I hate sports."

"Oh. Sorry for you. Sports is good. Keep fit. You should try."

The sour man who was interviewing my sister exited his office, Galina following him, looking calm and steady. I stood up. The sour man with the ugly brown tie gave me a look and then went into the next office to talk to Arvy.

"Did you make good answers?" I asked my sister.

"I told him the truth and nothing but the truth."

We both looked at the angry big woman. She finally answered her phone. I draped an arm around my sister and led her to a water fountain.

"I tell you watch Perry Mason be good. Know good lawyer-speak."

Galina smiled as she filled up a pointy paper cup with

water. "Stan, you should go. This is going to take a couple more hours at least. They have about five hundred questions." She paused to drink. "They ask about the number of windows in our bedroom, what our Wi-Fi password is, and do we have any siblings. So many nosy questions! I told him if he wished to see my sibling, just look out in the office. He's that massive Russian in the dark suit wearing a dopey smile."

"My smile is dopey with love."

"Yeah, I know." She lifted to her toes to press her chilly lips to my cheek. "Go home. Rest. You have to face Philadelphia for the first round of the playoffs in two days."

"Dieter say Trent's *babushka* make voodoo doll for each Railer." That worried me. Russians are superstitious. We never shake hands over a threshold, whistle indoors, sit at a corner table, and never wish someone a happy birthday prematurely. I spat three times over my shoulder. Big Angry Woman glowered at me. Galina giggled into her water cup.

"Stan, voodoo dolls are silly. Go home. Snuggle with Noah and Erik. I'll call when we're done."

"You come for dinner? Mama is making stroganoff with *vatrushka* for dessert. I have vodka for celebrating good green card day."

"I'm going to be so fat now that Mama is here." Galina sighed. I patted my stomach and nodded. "We'll be there as soon as we're done here. Go."

I gave her a look.

"Go! I can sit and read. Go. Shoo."

"Okay, I go."

She nodded at the door. When I stepped out onto the street, I was surprised to see Erik waiting for me. He looked so good leaning against our car, a warm spring breeze pushing a few curls into his eyes.

"Why you here?" I strolled over to him and ran my hand down his arm.

"Arvy texted me to come get you. Said they're suffering through the interview that may never end and you were driving the office workers crazy."

I looked back at the tall government office. "Me? I no drive crazy." My gaze went to my betrothed. "Do I make crazy?"

"I'm crazy in love with you. Does that count?"

My heart stuttered a bit. I took his hand and pressed a kiss to the knuckles, each one. Right on the street in downtown Harrisburg.

"It counts most big."

The End

Next for the Railers

Last Defense (Harrisburg Railers Hockey #5)

A hockey player with a medical secret, meets the owner of a no kill shelter. Two men afraid to feel, have to make choices that could end up breaking down their defenses and leading them back to love.

Every time Max Van Hellren steps on the ice he knows it could be his last time. At thirty he's past his hockey prime but he's also hiding a life-threatening injury that private doctors warn could kill him. This is his last season, and there's a chance he could lift the Stanley Cup after fourteen years in the NHL. He just needs to stay safe and healthy; difficult when he's known for his heavy hitting and with a propensity for dropping the gloves and putting his body in the way of pucks to keep his team safe.

A one night stand with a sexy man was just what he needed, dangerous and hot, but what if it turned into more? Would he actually have to share the secrets he so desperately tries to hide?

Ben Worthington had it all. A fulfilling job running the CrossRoads Shelter, his loving aunts, and a husband that understood his devotion to animals. Then, the love of his life left him, succumbing so quickly to an unexpected sickness that Ben never had time to say goodbye. The violent loss scarred him.

Unable to move past his fears, he moves from lonely encounter to lonely encounter, slaking a desperate need that is eating away at him, but never making a connection that could lead him back into love. One night with Max makes him want more, but will giving into the temptation open the door to feelings he can't contain?

Can these two broken men ever find a way to be together?

Hockey Series' from RJ Scott & V.L. Locey

Harrisburg Railers

Owatonna U Hockey

Arizona Raptors

Boston Rebels

LA Storm

Chesterford Coyotes - Young Adult

Free Reads

Please note - in all of these free stories, there will be some spoilers for the main series books.

Railers Short Stories

Volume 1 | Volume 2

LA Storm

Sparkle

The Colts - AHL Short Stories

Pucks & Percentages

Breakaway

Making the Save

Standalone

Waiting for Christmas

When hockey wunderkind Tennant Rowe meets his new coach, he knows he's in trouble. Jared Madsen is nine years older than Tennant, impossibly attractive, and — worst of all — his brother's off-limits best friend. Is their chemistry worth the risk?

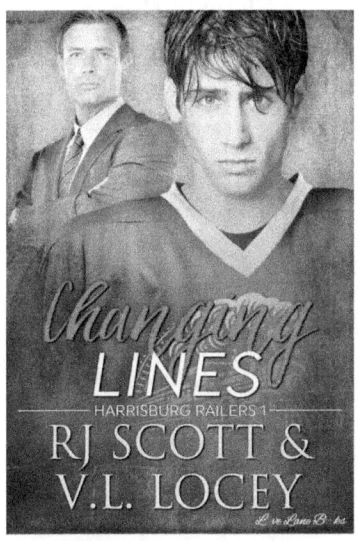

Changing Lines (Railers 1)

Can Tennant show Jared that age is just a number, and that love is all that matters?

The Rowe Brothers are famous hockey hotshots, but as the youngest of the trio, Tennant has always had to play against his brothers' reputations. To get out of their shadows, and against their advice, he accepts a trade to the Harrisburg Railers, where he runs into Jared Madsen. Mads is an old family friend and his brother's one-time teammate. Mads is Tennant's new coach. And Mads is the sexiest thing he's ever laid eyes on.

Jared Madsen's hockey career was cut short by a fault in his heart, but coaching keeps him close to the game. When Ten is traded to the team, his carefully organized world is thrown into chaos. Nine years his junior and his best friend's brother, he knows Ten is strictly off-limits, but as soon as he sees Ten's moves, on and off the ice, he knows that his heart could get him into trouble again.

Changing Lines

Harrisburg Railers (Hockey Romance)

1. Changing Lines
2. First Season
3. Deep Edge
4. Poke Check
5. Last Defense
6. Goal Line
7. Neutral Zone
8. Hat Trick
9. Save The Date
10. Baby Makes Three
11. Rivals
12. Perfect Gifts
13. Family First

Railers Volume 1 | Railers Volume 2 | Railers Volume 3 | Railers Volume 4

Meet the men of Owatonna University's hockey team

Ryker (Owatonna U, 1)

Ryker

Ryker is hockey royalty, Jacob is a poor country boy. Can two vastly different people find common ground and become the men they want to be?

Ryker comes from a long line of championship-winning hockey players. Playing college hockey to develop his game is his only focus, and nothing will stand in the way of him working to become the best player. He has no room for relationships, people who point out his flaws, or anyone who calls him on his dreams. He certainly has no place for love, and meeting Jacob is nothing but a useful distraction on the side. After all trying to get his Owatonna Eagles teammate into bed is less work and more play. When tragedy rocks his family, his charmed life crumbles, and the only person he can turn to is the same one who claims to hate him.

Jacob Benson has only known hard work and stifling conservative values his whole life. Born and raised in the small rural community of Eden Crossing, Minnesota, he's the only son of a hard-working but struggling dairy farming family. Jacob is using his skills in hockey to finance his way to an agricultural science degree. These four years at Owatonna U. will probably be the only time he has to enjoy life, gain acceptance about his sexuality, and live openly before his inevitable return to the farm. Running into a pretty rich boy like Ryker Madsen is putting a damper on his enjoyment of life away from home. Ryker's flip, conceited, carefree attitude grates on Jacob's every nerve. So why, if Ryker is everything he dislikes, does he want nothing more than to explore the sinful dreams that his annoying teammate stars in every night?

Ryker

Owatonna U Hockey (Hockey Romance)

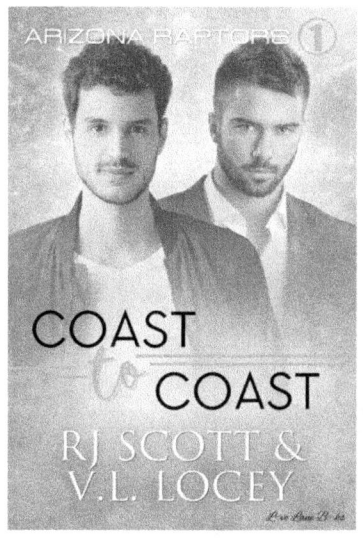

Coast to Coast (Arizona Raptors 1)

Coast To Coast

When opposites attract, this bottom-of-the-league team will never be the same again.

A stipulation in his father's will forces Mark back into the arms of a family that disowned him and leaves him one-third owner of a hockey team facing financial ruin. He doesn't even watch hockey, let alone like it, and wants nothing more than to head back to New York. Then there's the new coach, a stubborn, opinionated, irritating man with superiority issues and questionable music taste. Butting heads with Rowen becomes the new normal, but it comes with passionate debate and an all-consuming lust.

Challenged to rebuild one of the worst teams in the league into a future cup contender, Rowen can't pass up the opportunity. Never in his twenty years of hockey has he ever seen a team managed so badly or coached players overflowing with resentment and bigotry. Yet there's something about this team and this city that compels him to roll up his sleeves and start dismantling. If only Mark, one of three siblings who now own the Raptors, wasn't so damned rock-headed yet so damned appealing his job might be easier. It doesn't look like either is willing to give in, but one night in a dark, desert hotel changes everything.

Coast To Coast

―――――――

Arizona Raptors (Hockey Romance)

1. Coast To Coast
2. Across the Pond
3. Shadow and Light
4. Sugar and Ice
5. School and Rock

Boston Rebels

Top Shelf (Boston Rebels 1)

Acting on the attraction to his best friend's brother has always been off the table for Xander until a passionate hookup with Mason at a beach resort begins a love affair that burns long after summer ends.

Mason specializes in assisting same-sex couples on their journey to becoming parents and fighting every rule that blocks his way in the stuck-in-the-past agency that hired him. Living in his brother's pool house is rent-free, and every cent he earns he saves for his dream—that one day he'd have his own company helping others. The downside is that he has to see his annoying brother every day, the upside is that his brother's teammates from the Boston Rebels make regular visits. The eye candy that passes Mason's window is almost enough to make him consider dating a hockey player, but not just any player though. Ever since Xander —his brother's childhood friend—came out as gay at a press conference, Mason's puppy love has turned into a burning attraction he can no longer ignore.

Hockey has been one of Xander's main focuses since he was old enough to balance on skates. Well, hockey and Mason Kingsley, but Mason was always unattainable. Now that he's about to see thirty candles on his birthday cake and is no longer hiding the fact he's gay, he's ready to find a soul mate to make his life complete. A summer vacation is just what he needs to have time to think, but when the Boston Rebels arriving in paradise with Mason in tow, thinking is the last thing he needs. One torrid night under a balmy moon and rules about not messing with his best friend's brother vanish on a warm, tropical breeze.

Summer romances don't generally last past Labor Day, but with the new season about to begin Xander and Mason are going to have to face the world and decide if their love is real enough to withstand everything.

Boston Rebels

Lost In Boston (Free Prequel Novella)

1. Top Shelf
2. Back Check
3. Snowed
4. Royal Lines
5. Blade
6. Rental

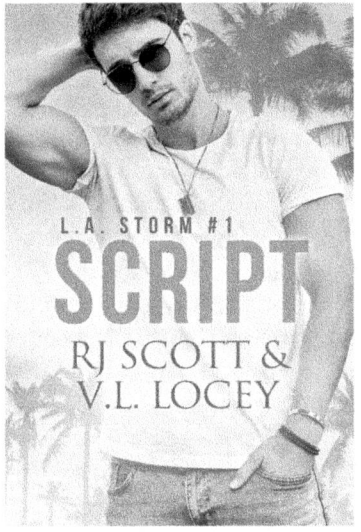

Script (LA Storm, 1)

Script

Hollywood A-lister Finn might be Canadian, but he needs Cameron to show him how to hockey.

Actor Finn Kerrigan is at a crossroads. After growing up a soap star, then starring in a hugely successful trilogy of action movies, he's finally given the chance to read a heartfelt and passionate script that could change his life forever. The role would be enough for people to see him as a serious actor, and maybe even win him an award or two (and no, a golden raspberry award for his action movies doesn't count). Once established as a serious actor he's sure he can come out of the closet and finally live his truth. When he lies to get the part of a hockey player on a struggling team, he suddenly has nowhere to hide. He might be Canadian, but the last time he skated he was ten, and no, he doesn't have hockey in his blood. With only a month until filming starts, he about to be exposed, but partnered with a player who's supposed to be giving him tips, he doesn't realize how many of his secrets will come to light. Falling in lust, one heated kiss at a time, is inevitable, but giving Cameron up at the end of the shoot could break his heart.

Cameron Chavkin is the face of the LA Storm. And the body, and the hair, and the smile. He's at the prime of his career, men and women want to be with him, and he's skating better than he ever has before. His house sits next to a famous rock star's mansion, his garage is filled with expensive cars, and he's even been asked to mentor a once-famous actor in a new hockey movie. Life is pretty sweet. Until the bad boy of hockey meets Finn, a man on the edge with more secrets than Cameron has endorsements. Knowing better than to get involved, Cameron is swept up despite himself, and when it's time to say goodbye to the Storm's most eligible bachelor is finding it hard to follow the script.

Script

LA Storm

Off The Ice (Chesterford Coyotes, 1)

Off The Ice

A coming-of-age love story with high school, hockey rivalry, friendship, family, and coming out.

Soren's life changes in an instant when he and his younger brother are adopted by hockey royalty. Making sense of his new life is hard enough, but when he's enrolled in a private school it means facing a whole new set of problems. Navigating friendship, family, and hockey is one thing, but being attracted to the boy who vexes him is a whole new thing.

Felix has a reputation to protect. He's the kid who seems to have everything but looks can be deceiving. Spinning lies about his perfect life, he's created a fantasy world that even he has started to believe. Only, it's not long before everything crumbles, all of his pretty lies are revealed, and only his closest rival sees through his pain and stands by him.

Fighting is easy, friendship is hard, but love is everything.

Off The Ice

Chesterford Coyotes

1. Off The Ice
2. On Thin Ice
3. *Dance on Ice*

Also By RJ Scott

For a full list of ebooks and links please scan the code above or
visit rjscott.co.uk/rjbooks

Meet RJ Scott

RJ discovered romance in books at a very young age and realized that if there wasn't romance on the page, she could create it in her head. With over one hundred and fifty books published, she is a full time author of gay romance.

She lives and works out of her home in the beautiful English countryside, spends her spare time reading, watching films, and enjoying time with her family.

The last time she had a week's break from writing she didn't like it one little bit and has yet to meet a box of chocolates she couldn't defeat.

www.rjscott.co.uk | rj@rjscott.co.uk

NEWSLETTER - rjscott.co.uk/rjnews

facebook.com/author.rjscott

x.com/Rjscott_author

instagram.com/rjscott_author

amazon.com/author/rj-scott

bookbub.com/authors/rj-scott

goodreads.com/rjscott

pinterest.com/rjscottauthor

Also By VL Locey

For a full list of ebooks and links please scan the code above or visit vllocey.com/stories-from-vl-locey

Meet V.L. Locey

V.L. Locey loves worn jeans, yoga, belly laughs, walking, reading and writing lusty tales, Greek mythology, the New York Rangers, comic books, and coffee.

(Not necessarily in that order.)

She shares her life with her husband, her daughter, one dog, two cats, a flock of assorted domestic fowl, and two Jersey steers.

When not writing spicy romances, she enjoys spending her day with her menagerie in the rolling hills of Pennsylvania with a cup of fresh java in hand.

vllocey.com
vicki@vllocey.com

Newsletter - vllocey.com/newsletter

facebook.com/V.L.Locey
x.com/vllocey
instagram.com/vl_locey
bookbub.com/authors/v-l-locey
goodreads.com/vllocey
pinterest.com/vllocey

Meet V.L. Locey

V.L. Locey loves worn jeans, yoga, belly laughs, walking, reading and writing lusty tales, Greek mythology, the New York Rangers, comic books, and coffee.

(Not necessarily in that order.)

She shares her life with her husband, her daughter, one dog, two cats, a flock of assorted domestic fowl, and two Jersey steers.

When not writing spicy romances, she enjoys spending her day with her menagerie in the rolling hills of Pennsylvania with a cup of fresh java in hand.

vllocey.com
vicki@vllocey.com

Newsletter - vllocey.com/newsletter

facebook.com/V.L.Locey

x.com/vllocey

instagram.com/vl_locey

bookbub.com/authors/v-l-locey

goodreads.com/vllocey

pinterest.com/vllocey

www.ingramcontent.com/pod-product-compliance
Lightning Source LLC
Chambersburg PA
CBHW060437180626
46817CB00007B/2859